Nightmare in 3-D

Wes buys one of those cool 3-D posters, hoping the image will come popping out at him. And boy, does it ever! It's a giant, hungry, drooling praying mantis—that can't wait to get its pincers on Wes!

The Bugman Lives!

Janet has a job mowing lawns for the summer. Sounds like easy money. Until she mows over a grave on one of her customer's lawns. It's the grave of the Bugman of Shadyside—a horrible monster who is half man, half bug. Soon Janet realizes that the Bugman is awake! And he wants Janet to join his buggy family!

Halloween Bugs Me!

All Greg wants is to collect more Halloween candy than his rival, Derek. But when a strange old lady gives him a magic bag, he doesn't just get more candy. He gets more cats, more dogs, more bugs—and more TROUBLE!

Also from R.L. Stine

The Beast®
The Beast® 2

Available from MINSTREL Books

R·L·STINE'S
GHOSTS OF FEAR STREET ®

CREEPY COLLECTION #4:
BIG BAD BUGS

A Parachute Book

A
MINSTREL ®
BOOK

Published by POCKET BOOKS
New York   London   Toronto   Sydney   Tokyo   Singapore

These titles were previously published individually.

A Minstrel Paperback published by
POCKET BOOKS, a division of Simon & Schuster Inc.
1230 Avenue of the Americas, New York, NY 10020

Nightmare in 3-D copyright © 1996 by Parachute Press, Inc.
The Bugman Lives! copyright © 1996 by Parachute Press, Inc.
Halloween Bugs Me! copyright © 1997 by Parachute Press, Inc.

NIGHTMARE IN 3-D WRITTEN BY GLORIA HATRICK
THE BUGMAN LIVES! WRITTEN BY CAROL GORMAN
HALLOWEEN BUGS ME! WRITTEN BY BARBARA JOYCE

ISBN: 0-671-02295-4

First Minstrel Books paperback printing August 1998

10 9 8 7 6 5 4 3 2 1

FEAR STREET is a registered trademark of Parachute Press, Inc.

A MINSTREL BOOK and colophon are registered trademarks of Simon & Schuster Inc.

Front cover illustration by Mark Garro

Printed in the U.S.A.

CREEPY COLLECTION #4:
BIG BAD BUGS

GHOSTS of FEAR STREET ®

NIGHTMARE
IN 3-D

1

"You have to cross your eyes, Wes."

"No, you don't, Wes. You just have to cross one eye."

"That's wrong, you jerk. Just stare at the two dots until they look like three dots, Wes. Then look at the whole picture and you'll see it."

The "it" everybody was talking about was a stereogram—one of those pictures with a hidden 3-D image. Mr. Gosling showed us one in our sixth-grade science class today. We're studying optics and learning about how we see things.

It was lunchtime now, and my best friend,

Lauren, and two other kids in my class were trying to give me tips on how to see stereograms. But I knew they were wasting their time.

I mushed my gravy into my mashed potatoes and slid the carrots to one side of my plate. The carrots in the school cafeteria are always soggy.

"It's no use," I said, pushing my glasses up. "I just can't see 3-D."

"You can, Wes," Lauren insisted. "It just takes some practice. You'll get it."

That's what I like about Lauren. She thinks positive. Another thing I like about her is her bright blue eyes. They look so cool under her black bangs.

"What will Wes get?" Cornelia Phillips demanded, shoving in next to me at the table.

Cornelia is one of the horrible twins who live next door to my family. Her horrible sister, Gabriella, strutted up right behind her.

Gabriella slid her tray across the table, then sat down, too. As if we'd invited them or something.

"What will you get, Wes?" Gabriella repeated. They're both so nosy.

Then, while they waited for my answer, they both twirled their long blond ponytails. They wear

2

them coming out of the sides of their heads, only on different sides so you can tell them apart. Otherwise they're alike in every gross detail. They even snort alike when they laugh.

And I hear them snorting a lot because, as I said, the twins live next door to me—on Fear Street. Everyone has stories about the scary things that happen on Fear Street. But if you ask me, the twins are the scariest things on the block!

They're worse than the ghost that everyone says plays hide-and-seek with you in the woods—and tries to steal your body. Or that ghostly substitute teacher my friend Zack had.

I call the twins Corny and Gabby. Perfect names. Corny's always playing dumb practical jokes, mostly on me. She'll do anything to make me look like a total idiot.

And Gabby's always talking. She's the biggest gossip at Shadyside Middle School. And guess who most of her stories are about? That's right—me. Wes Parker.

"What will Wes get?" the twins demanded together, their voices growing higher and higher.

I tried to ignore them. That's what Lauren always tells me to do. I stared down at my plate and mashed my potatoes around some more.

When no one answered, Corny finally changed the subject.

"Did you ever see anything grosser than that cow eye Mr. Gosling dissected?" she asked. Then she wrinkled her nose and gazed at everyone. Waiting for an answer.

"We're eating lunch, Cornelia," Lauren reminded her.

"Yeah, I thought it was going to squirt right off the table when he cut it open," Gabby added, ignoring Lauren.

Lauren and I groaned and dropped our forks. The twins snorted together.

"Hi, Chad." Corny waved at Chad Miller at the next table. He's one of the cool kids. Chad didn't even glance at her.

"Hey, he smiled at you!" Gabby said. She twirled her hair with one hand and stuffed her face full of potatoes with the other.

Lauren rolled her eyes.

"Wow. This table is bor-ring!" Corny groaned.

"Yeah," Gabby agreed. She reached into her backpack and pulled out a poster. She spread it out on the table, practically pushing my tray off.

Oh, no, I thought. Another stereogram. The other kids leaned over to study it.

"Can you see it, Wes?" Corny asked in a fake sweet voice.

She knew I couldn't. I never can see them. But I stared at the poster and tried hard to see the hidden image.

No use.

"Uh-uh," I admitted. I felt really stupid. The twins can always do that to me. "I can't see it. I just can't see it."

Corny leaned across my tray. She was right in my face. "Well, then, you'd better eat your carrots."

Gabby rolled the poster up and both twins left, whispering to each other and snorting some more.

"They think they're a riot," I grumbled. "Eat my carrots. Very funny."

I gazed down at my carrots.

Gasped in disbelief.

And then let out a scream that shook the room.

2

My carrots stared back at me!

An enormous eyeball poked up from the middle of them.

I shoved my chair away from the table. It caught on a loose floor tile and flipped over backward—with me in it.

Then someone started to clap—slowly. I gazed up. It was Corny. She wore a big grin on her face.

Then Gabby joined in. With the same slow, loud clap.

Lauren helped me up. "You okay?" she asked.

I nodded and straightened my chair.

The whole cafeteria was clapping and laughing now. Even the cool kids.

I tried to smile as I sat back down.

I picked up my fork and forced myself to prod the cow eye. It rolled into the mashed potatoes.

"It's fake," I said to Lauren through clenched teeth. "It's only plastic." Then I began to stand.

"Where are you going?" she asked.

"I am going to get up—and kill the twins," I answered.

"Forget it," Lauren replied, tugging me back down. "It was just another one of the twins' stupid jokes. You have to ignore them."

I glanced around, searching the cafeteria for them, but they had vanished. "I'm not going to ignore them. Not this time," I said through clenched teeth. "This time I'm going to get even."

I still felt upset when school let out. Lauren and I decided to hang around in the Old Village before heading home.

"I don't care what you say, Lauren. This time I'm going to get back at the twins."

"What are you going to do?" she asked. "You're too cool to play any of their stupid jokes."

"I don't know . . ." I stopped short in the middle of the sidewalk. I felt as if someone had jerked me back by the hair. "Look!" I said, pointing into Sal's Five-and-Ten.

The twins' stereogram hung in the window. The one they showed us at lunch.

A sign over it read: MYSTERY STEREOGRAM— FIND THE HIDDEN IMAGE AND WIN A PRIZE!

"That's it!" I cried.

"What are you talking about?" Lauren asked.

"That poster is the same one the twins had at lunch," I explained. "So they must be trying to win the prize. If I can figure out the poster before they do, it will be the perfect revenge."

"All right! Let's go in!" Lauren cheered, leading the way into Sal's.

The ancient wooden floor creaked under our feet as we stepped inside. "It smells funny in here," I whispered. "Old and musty. And a little like rotting eggs."

"Whew," Lauren breathed. "It's really hot, too." She unzipped her jacket.

We wandered up and down rows of metal tables. Each was divided into sections by pieces of cardboard. None of the stuff seemed organized. Plastic

8

dolls sat next to piles of pot holders. Tubes of lipstick leaned against a stack of pocketknives.

And everything loose. Nothing came in boxes or wrapped in plastic.

"This store is really old and really weird," Lauren commented. She opened a lipstick to check the color. It was half used. Yuck.

We moved on.

Some old music played in the background. I recognized it. It sounded like the kind my grandfather plays when we visit him. Big band music, he calls it. It floated from a huge old radio.

I'd almost forgotten all about the Mystery Stereogram when a guy popped up from behind the back counter.

Lauren and I leaped back in surprise. He seemed to appear out of nowhere.

That must be Sal, I realized.

He dressed all in black and his hair was greased back. And he had an incredible mustache. It curled up and around to his cheeks. Really weird. But it wasn't the weirdest thing about him.

The weirdest thing was his eyes. They were enormous and watery, like the cow eye in class. And they bulged out from his eye sockets.

9

I took a step back and nearly knocked over a basket full of Mystery Stereograms. I lifted one out and unrolled it. "I . . . I want one of these," I said.

Sal blinked. "Oh. That," he snarled.

"Uh, I was wondering—how come there's a prize?"

"Is it a special kind of stereogram or something?" Lauren added.

Sal shook his head impatiently. "That has nothing to do with me." Then he turned his back to us.

I cleared my throat. "But it's in your window."

"Yes." He sighed, then spun around to face us again. "It *is* in my window. But I didn't put it there. The poster company did. They are offering the prize. I allowed them to hang it up. I thought it might bring in customers. No one wants to shop in five-and-tens anymore. Everyone is at the mall."

When he said "mall," he curled his lip and rolled his huge eyes. "I can't compete."

Lauren spread the poster out on the dusty glass counter.

I stared hard at its billions of tiny fluorescent dots. They were yellow, green, orange, and pink. But I couldn't see a picture inside it.

"I see only dots, Lauren," I admitted.

Lauren moved closer to the poster, then backed away. Then she smiled. "No big deal, Wes. Neither can I."

Sal reached out and grabbed the poster. "Good. Then that's settled." He started to shove it under the counter.

"But I want it," I protested. I had to get my revenge on the two monsters of Fear Street. "I have to figure out how to see it."

Sal frowned. "You can see it. You need only three things to see a stereogram."

I waited, holding my breath. Finally, someone was going to tell me the secret.

"You need a right eye. A left eye. And a brain." He smiled for the first time. He had big teeth, like a horse.

Some secret, I thought. Did he think I'd been trying to see stereograms without my brain? I handed my money over to Sal.

"You better be careful," he warned as he rang up the sale on his noisy old-fashioned cash register.

"Be careful of what?" Lauren asked.

Sal moved around the counter to stand close to me. He placed his face right up to mine and opened his eyelids wide. His big eyes bulged out

11

more than ever now. I could see all these tiny red veins running through his eyeballs.

I tried to back away, but the basket of rolled-up posters stood directly behind me.

Sal stared at me so hard I felt as though he had X-ray vision. *"You* have the power to see more than most of us," he said in a creepy whisper.

I slid sideways to move away from him. This guy was beyond weird. "No, uh, I can't really see well at all. That's why I wear glasses."

"I am not talking about twenty-twenty eyesight. I am talking about true vision. *The power to see."*

He hissed the word *see* and his eyes bulged out even farther.

"Uh, it's getting kind of late," Lauren said. "We'd better get going, Wes." She smiled nervously.

I grabbed the poster from Sal. Then Lauren and I practically jogged down the aisle to the door. I gripped the door handle and pulled the door open—but a huge hand flew over my shoulder and slammed it shut.

I spun around.

Sal stared hard at me.

"Remember," he said again in that scary whisper. "*You* have the power to see. And some things are better left in two dimensions."

Lauren and I opened the door and hurried onto the sidewalk.

What did he mean by that? I wondered.

Why was he trying to scare me?

3

I was still trying to figure out what Sal meant when I reached home. *"You* have the power to see." Why did he keep saying that to me—and not to Lauren?

And why did he warn me to be careful?

I threw my jacket over one of the kitchen chairs and spread the Mystery Stereogram out on the table. I pinned it down with the salt and pepper shakers.

I stared and stared. "You have the power to see," Sal's words repeated in my head.

Ha! What did he know?

I couldn't see a thing.

I rubbed my eyes, wiped my glasses on my flannel shirt, and tried again.

I gazed at the poster close up.

I stepped back and stared at it from far away.

Close up again.

Then far away.

"What on earth are you doing?" Mom asked as she walked through the kitchen door, struggling with two huge bags of groceries. "Didn't you hear me honking the horn?"

"No. Sorry, Mom." Boy, I must have really been concentrating!

I went out to the car for the last two bags of groceries. As I entered the kitchen, Clawd, our cat, streaked between my legs and bolted through the kitchen and into the living room. He nearly sent me flying.

Outside I could hear a dog's annoying yipping. It was Fluffums, the twins' nasty little dog.

Fluffums attacks Clawd every chance he gets. He hates Clawd. It figures.

"Look what I bought," I said as Mom started unpacking the groceries. "It's a poster. I got it at the weird five-and-ten store in the Old Village."

15

Mom stopped and sniffed. "What's that horrible smell?"

I sniffed. "I think it's my poster. It smells like the store."

"Sal's Five-and-Ten?" she asked. "I haven't been in that strange little store in years."

"It's strange all right," I said. "Especially Sal." I sat down at the table. "Take a look at the poster."

Mom glanced at it.

"Cool, huh?" I asked.

"It really stinks," Mom said, covering her nose.

"Yeah, I know. But look at it, Mom. It's called a stereogram. And if you stare at it the right way, you can see a three-dimensional image hidden in it."

Mom folded a bag and leaned over the poster. "All I can see are a bunch of colored dots."

As Mom peered closer at it, my little sister, Vicky, ran into the kitchen. "Hey, Mom! Did you buy Froot Loops? Can I have a bowl now? Hey — is that 3-D?"

Vicky always does that. Asks a whole load of questions, one on top of the other. She doesn't even give you time to answer.

"Yes, no, and yes," Mom said. She's used to Vicky and her questions.

But Vicky wasn't even listening. She was staring at my poster. "Cool," she said, pushing her glasses up her nose. "There's one of these on the back of my cereal box. I'll show you." She reached up to the counter cabinet and pulled the box down.

We all studied it. It had lots of red and blue squiggles.

"It says there's a mouse hidden in the picture," Vicky said, "and I can see it. It's a big mouse."

I stared at the box. All I could see were the squiggles. "Hey, how do you do that?" I asked. I couldn't believe my little sister could see it and I couldn't.

Vicky shrugged. "I kind of cross one eye, like this." She peered up, and sure enough, behind her glasses I could see one eye gazing straight at me. The other was staring at her nose.

"Stop that, Vicky!" Mom exclaimed. "Your eyes will stay like that."

Vicky uncrossed her eye. "It says on the cereal box there are other ways to do it, too."

I read the directions off the back of the box.

17

"Press your nose against the picture. Then, very slowly, pull it away. Don't blink. As you look deeply into the picture, a 3-D image will appear!"

I tried it. No luck. Just a bunch of fat squiggles.

Mom tried it. "I feel silly." She laughed. She slowly pulled the cereal box away from her face. "No. Wait. I've got it! There is a mouse! He's eating something!"

I couldn't believe it. They had to be teasing me.

"Here. Try it again, Wes," Mom said to me. "It really works."

I held the box close, pressing it against my nose. The tiny red and blue designs were a blur. I pulled the box away slowly, my eyes wide open. Not blinking.

But I could feel my eyes struggling to refocus. And that's exactly what they did.

I was staring at squiggles.

No mouse.

No 3-D image.

I felt totally frustrated. "Okay," I said, holding the box up in front of them. "If both of you can see it so well, what's the mouse eating?"

Mom and Vicky peered at the picture together.

"Come on," I said. "What's it eating?"

"Swiss cheese," they sang out together.

18

I slammed the box on the table. "I'll do it," I silently promised myself. "Even if it kills me."

Clawd wandered back into the kitchen and jumped onto my lap. He tilted his head as he stared at the cereal box. Then he took a swipe at it, knocking the box over.

"I don't believe it!" I shouted. "Even the cat can see 3-D! Wait a second. If you're all so smart, tell me what's in this picture," I commanded.

I stood up and stabbed my finger at the Mystery Stereogram. Clawd jumped down and darted to a corner in the kitchen.

Mom and Vicky studied the poster. I could see Vicky crossing one eye again.

Mom shook her head. "No. I can't do that one."

Vicky's face was practically touching it. "Yuck!" she cried, backing away. "This thing smells like something rotten."

"Hah! You can't see it, either!"

"Let Clawd try," Vicky suggested. She carried it over to Clawd's corner, where he was licking a paw.

She held the poster up in front of him. He stopped licking his paw, but for a second he didn't put it down. He just kind of froze in place. And stared.

Then all his fur stood out. He looked as if he'd been in the clothes dryer or something. He arched his back and opened his mouth so wide that I could see every single one of his teeth. Even the ones all the way in the back.

Then he hissed and tore through the catflap faster than I'd ever seen him move.

Vicky shrugged. "Guess he didn't like it."

I rolled up the poster and said I was going upstairs to my room to do my homework. But instead of studying, I took my Shaquille O'Neal poster down from the wall by my bed and hung up the Mystery Stereogram in its place.

Now I could stare at it last thing at night, first thing in the morning.

I was determined to see 3-D. I was determined to win the contest.

I was going to beat those horrible twins.

"I'll start practicing this minute," I said aloud. "Homework will have to wait."

I sat cross-legged on my bed. First I'll try Vicky's way, I thought. The one-eye-crossed method.

But I quickly found out that I'm not very good at crossing one eye. I can cross two okay. But I could tell that crossing one at a time was going to take a lot of practice. And I didn't have that much time—if I was going to beat the twins.

Then I did what the cereal box said. I moved up real close to the poster. The tiny bright dots grew into a blur. Then I slowly inched backward on my bed.

I kept my eyes wide open.

I didn't blink.

My eyes started to burn. They were trying hard to focus.

I backed up a little more.

A little more.

Then—I fell out of bed.

"Wesley? What are you doing up there?" Dad was home from work.

"Just practicing my kung fu," I joked.

"Well, cut it out." Not a joke.

Clawd popped his head in the doorway.

"Come here, Clawd." I patted the bed.

The cat took a small step into the room. Then he noticed the poster. His ears flattened. His eyes narrowed. Then he turned and ran.

I flopped down on my bed and slipped off my glasses. I rubbed my eyes. They felt tired. I gazed

21

blankly at my wallpaper. The same wallpaper I've had since I was three years old. Rows and rows of toy soldiers.

Then I saw it! I couldn't believe it!

I rubbed my eyes and stared again.

Yes! One of the soldiers was moving. He was marching.

Marching off the wallpaper.

Marching toward me.

4

I bolted straight up in bed and jerked my head from the wallpaper.

I felt so dizzy. Did I really see what I thought I saw? Only one way to find out.

I slowly turned to face the wall and . . .

Nothing.

The toy soldier stood flat and still.

No marching.

No 3-D.

Same as always.

But I had seen a soldier move. I knew it.

I rubbed my eyes hard and concentrated—this time on the Mystery Stereogram. I felt my eyes relax.

Slowly all the tiny dots began to swirl. Orange, green, yellow, and pink dots flowed around the poster. Like lava spewing from a volcano.

I started to feel a little sick. The way I feel on a Ferris wheel. But I kept staring, not daring to blink.

I felt myself falling forward. As if something were trying to pull me into the poster. I grabbed a fistful of covers with each hand to anchor myself. But I didn't blink.

The dots spun around even faster. They seemed to surround me, trying to suck me in with the power of a huge vacuum cleaner.

Still—I didn't blink. And now the dots were forming a shape. A tree?

Yes! A tree!

And then I saw something in the tree. A bird? No, not a bird.

Something with a really long, skinny body. And two huge feelers.

And a big triangular head. And eyes! Two huge black eyes.

And finally I could see two long front legs

24

forming out of the dots. Two long legs with pincers on the ends!

A praying mantis!

That was it! I could see it! I could see in 3-D!

A praying mantis! Now I could claim the prize. I beat the twins!

I tried to blink, but my eyelids felt glued open. I couldn't break away.

I noticed even more details.

The mantis's jaws were large and powerful.

The eyes were wet and shiny.

It looked alive!

Something brushed against my neck. Then I felt tiny legs crawling over my cheek.

I dropped the covers and brushed the side of my face. My fingers touched something soft and fluttery. Ewww!

I swatted at it. I jerked my head back as it darted past my eyes.

A moth?

A sigh of relief escaped my lips. Get a grip, Wes, I told myself. This 3-D thing is making you jittery.

I watched the moth flutter around the room. And circle back. And hover in front of the poster.

Then something else caught my eye.

Nah. It couldn't be. No way.

25

I thought I saw the mantis twitch. I really *was* losing it.

I reached out and snatched the moth in midair. I held it in my fist. I could feel its wings beating against the palm of my hand.

Slowly I moved my fist to the left side of the poster.

Slowly I uncurled my fingers.

I could feel the moth crawl up my little finger. But I never tore my eyes from the mantis.

I watched it carefully.

I watched as it twisted its head to the left. I watched as it peered at the moth.

It peered at the moth!

The mantis really was alive!

Suddenly I heard Sal's words as clearly as if he stood in the room with me. "Some things are better left in two dimensions."

The moth flew from my hand and landed on the poster. Then it started crawling up the tree. Up to where the mantis lurked. Waiting.

I held my breath. My eyes began to water but I didn't dare blink. Not now.

The mantis's head moved slightly. Its feelers twitched. It held its front legs together. Just as if it were praying.

The moth climbed up the tree. Moved nearer and nearer to the mantis. Then one of the mantis's long front legs lashed out from the picture!

In one swift motion its huge pincers closed down on the moth and jerked it into the poster.

And I watched in horror as the mantis shoved the moth—wings and all—straight into its waiting mouth.

The mantis swallowed with a wet gulp.

Then its big eyes rolled hungrily toward me.

5

"Dinner!" Mom shouted from downstairs.

I blinked.

"Wes, are you coming?" Dad hollered.

"Uh, yeah," I croaked.

My pulse raced. Something tickled my forehead. I jerked my hand up to swipe at it. Only tiny beads of perspiration dripping down my face.

I slid away from the poster and tried to stand up. My knees shook so badly I had to sit back down on the bed.

But I didn't look at the poster again. I wasn't ready.

28

I fumbled for my glasses and put them on with trembling hands. Calm down, I told myself. Just calm down.

When my breathing began to slow and my hands stopped shaking, I knew I had to take another peek at the poster.

Okay, here I go, I told myself firmly, trying to build up my confidence.

I slowly turned to face the poster, and my gaze was met with . . .

Colored dots.

Only colored dots.

No mantis.

And no moth.

I tried to think of a logical explanation. That's what Mr. Gosling, my science teacher, always tells us to do. But I couldn't come up with one. I decided I had to tell Mom and Dad. They were logical. Usually.

I joined my family at the dinner table. Mom had made spaghetti and garlic toast. My favorite. Too bad I wasn't hungry.

"Pass the Parmesan cheese, please," Dad said. He smiled. "Hey, I'm a poet and I don't even know it!"

"But your feet show it. They're Longfellows,"

Vicky finished for him. It was a silly game they always played.

"Uh, something strange just happened in my bedroom," I began.

"Mom, what's for dessert?" Vicky asked. "Can I have some more milk?"

"Frozen yogurt. Yes," Mom said, reaching for the milk.

"Is there any more spaghetti?" Dad asked.

They weren't paying attention to me. I had to make them listen.

"Here you go," Mom said, passing the bowl.

"I think my 3-D poster is coming alive!" I blurted out. That ought to get them.

Dad raised his eyebrows. "What do you mean, Wes?" he asked as he twirled his fork on his spoon, winding the spaghetti.

I cleared my throat. "I found a praying mantis in my poster, and it ate a moth that was flying around in my room."

"Yuck!" Vicky uttered, spitting out a mouthful of spaghetti. "That's disgusting!"

"So is that," Dad warned Vicky. He pushed his glasses up on his nose. "Wes, you probably just stared at it too hard. Your eyes can do funny things when they're tired."

30

"No, you don't understand," I protested. "I saw—"

Yeoow! Clawd raced through the catflap at full speed with a high-pitched screech.

Right behind him came Fluffums.

Our eyes followed the two crazed animals, but no one at the table moved. I don't think any of us could believe it. Fluffums. In our house.

Then someone pounded on the kitchen door. "Give us our dog back!" I heard one of the twins yell.

Hah! As if we'd invited the furry little rat in! For a second I didn't know whether to chase after the animals or go to the door and tell them off.

"I'll get the door," my father said.

"Wes, find Clawd," Mom ordered.

I searched the downstairs. Clawd wasn't there. So I dashed upstairs. Now I could hear Clawd yowling and Fluffums yipping. The sounds were coming from my bedroom.

When I hit the top step I froze. An agonizing yelp of pain echoed in my ears.

I tore down the hall, straight for my room. The first thing I spotted was Clawd, perched on my tall dresser. His back was arched and his fur stood straight out.

I gazed around the room for Fluffums. I couldn't find him.

Then I heard whimpering from the corner. The dog cowered there, his ears and tail down, his little body trembling.

Before I could make a move, the twins barreled in.

"Where's Fluffums?" Corny demanded. She shoved me out of the way. In my own room!

"Look! There! In the corner!" Gabby shouted. "I'll get him." She pushed past me, too, and reached down for the dog.

He growled. "I hope he bites her," I muttered under my breath.

"What's the matter, little Fluffums?" Gabby cooed in baby talk.

Fluffums whined and backed farther into the corner.

"Did that nasty old cat tease you again?" Corny added. She glared at Clawd—then at me.

I scooped Clawd up off the dresser. He clung to my shoulder. "Ouch!" I cried out as his claws sunk right through my shirt. He was in a real panic.

"Nasty cat." Gabby sneered, petting her dog. "He even claws his owner."

"Only when he's scared to death," I shot back.

"Come on, Baby Fluffy," Corny crooned. She swept the furball into her arms. She held him cradled in front of her like a baby.

"Oh, no!" Gabby shouted, pointing to the dog. "Look at his side! There's a patch of fur missing!"

"It was torn out!" Corny exclaimed. "By that horrible cat."

I stared at the dog's side. There *was* some fur missing. "Are you sure it wasn't missing before?" I asked. "Maybe he's going bald or something."

The twins went ballistic.

"He's not going bald, you jerk. Your stupid cat attacked him!" Corny shouted.

"We're going to tell our parents," Gabby threatened. "They've got a lawyer and he'll sue you. You and your cat and your whole family."

They stomped out of my room.

I stroked Clawd behind the ears. "You didn't do that—did you, Clawd?" I whispered. "You wouldn't hurt a fly."

Clawd started to squirm out of my arms. I let him go. He charged out of the room.

My eyes moved across the room to the poster.

What was that spot on the front?

I walked over and touched it.

Then a cold chill ran down my body.

The spot—it was white and soft.

Furry.

A clump of Fluffum's fur!

But that was impossible!

How did it get there?

Did the praying mantis . . .

No! Impossible!

I sprinted out of my room to tell Mom and Dad.

But on the way downstairs I overheard Mom say something so awful I had to stop and listen.

"I can't imagine how Clawd would cope." Mom sounded sad. "He's not a house cat. He loves to curl up in the backyard. Don't you think it would be cruel to lock him inside?"

Dad didn't answer right away.

What is he waiting for? He knows Clawd would hate being cooped up in the house.

"We have to think about it," he said finally. "This dog and cat situation has been the cause of a lot of problems."

I felt my face get hot. I'll straighten this out, I decided. All I have to do is tell them that Clawd didn't touch the twins' dumb little dog. All I have to do is tell them that it was the mantis.

Yeah, right. A 3-D mantis. Like they'll really believe me. Anyway, they'd probably think I was making the whole thing up to get Clawd out of trouble.

I turned around and crept back up the stairs to my room. My eyes darted to the mystery poster hanging over my bed. No way did I want to go to sleep anywhere near that, I thought.

My fingers shook as I reached over the bed toward the poster. What if one of those sharp green pincers shot out and grabbed me?

I tugged all four thumbtacks out as fast as I could. Then I grabbed the poster and rolled it up—tight.

Whew! Getting it off the wall felt good. I put my Shaq poster back up and felt even better. Maybe everything would turn back to normal now.

I decided to put the poster in my closet. I stuck it behind one of my failures—the hula hoop. The twins were hula hoop champions—of course. I could never get that thing to stay up.

But I didn't fail with the poster, I reminded myself. I could claim the prize from the poster company. I'd won it fair and square. For once, I'd beaten the twin monsters of Fear Street!

I rummaged around in my top desk drawer and found a postcard. "It's a mantis," I wrote on the card. Then I addressed it to the poster company. I printed my name and address in one corner and stuck a stamp on the other.

I decided to mail the postcard right away. I jumped down the stairs two at a time, told my parents I'd be right back, and jogged to the mailbox on the corner.

As I dropped the postcard in, I breathed a sigh of relief. I'd solved the Mystery Stereogram and mailed in the answer. I was finished with the poster. I felt great!

I glanced over at the twins' house as I walked

back home. I couldn't wait to see their faces when my prize arrived.

I imagined their reaction again and again as I climbed the stairs to my room. I could hear their angry little squeals. I could see their faces getting all red and scrunched up.

I sat down to do my homework, and before I knew it, it was time for bed. I was so tired! What a day!

I placed my glasses on the small table next to my bed. Then I punched my pillow a few times and turned off the bedside light. I wanted to dream about the moment the twins realized I'd beaten them.

But I couldn't fall asleep.

What was that strange light?

I sat up and glanced around.

I saw a faint glow. It came from under the closet door.

Did I leave the light on in my closet when I put the poster away?

I threw back the covers to hop out of bed. But I stopped when I saw the crack under the door begin to glow brighter and brighter.

With my eyes trained on the strange glow, I reached back, fumbled for the lamp switch—and sent the lamp crashing to the floor. The lightbulb shattered into a million razor-sharp pieces.

I quickly turned back to the closet door—and gasped!

A few bright fluorescent dots floated out from beneath it.

They shimmered like lightning bugs. Green, pink, orange, and yellow lightning bugs. They circled slowly, chasing one another.

Huh? Am I seeing things? I wondered. I knelt on the edge of my bed. Were my eyes playing tricks on me the way Dad thought? Had I fooled around with 3-D too much?

More dots floated out. More and more and more. Thousands of the dots streamed from under the closet door.

They bounced off the walls.

Careened off the furniture.

They swirled in lazy circles.

I gaped at them, frozen in horror. In disbelief.

Swirling. Swirling.

And then, without warning, they started swirling around me!

And buzzing—an angry, grating buzz—the sound of a thousand hungry insects!

7

I pressed my hands against my ears as hard as I could, but I couldn't keep the noise out. I felt as if the buzzing dots were trapped inside my head. Crawling through my ears and behind my eyes.

The dots glowed brighter. They twirled around me faster and faster.

My eyes itched and burned. I wanted to rub them, but I was afraid to unblock my ears.

The itching spread through my entire body. Down my neck, my chest, around my back, over my arms and legs.

I squeezed into the corner of my bed. Then I quickly grabbed for my pillow and pulled it over my head.

I wanted to scream for help, but I was afraid to open my mouth. I was afraid the dots would fly inside me. Crawl down my throat and into my stomach.

A foul odor rose over my room. I could smell it through the pillow. Worse than a skunk or rotten eggs or spoiled milk.

My stomach lurched. My throat and nose burned. My entire body itched.

I had to do something!

I had to stop the swirling dots!

I released my grip on the pillow and grabbed my bedspread. I wound it around my arm. Then I dropped to my hands and knees and crawled toward the closet.

The buzzing grew almost unbearable without the pillow protecting my ears.

I forced myself to inch forward—until I reached the closet. The dots were still spilling out.

I shoved one edge of the blanket under the door. The dots kept coming. My fingers shook as I stuffed more of the blanket into the crack. I could feel the dots pushing against it. Struggling to get out.

I kept jamming the blanket under the door until it was wedged in tight. Then I backed up.

No light leaked from the closet.

I spun around.

All the dots in the room had disappeared.

I sat down carefully on the edge of my bed. I stared at the closet door. Waiting to see if the dots could escape my barricade.

I stared into the darkness for a long time. The room remained dark and silent.

The knots in my stomach disappeared. My hands fell open at my sides. I realized I'd been clenching my teeth, and I relaxed my jaws.

My breathing came slower and deeper. My eyes began drifting closed. I couldn't stay awake any longer. I crawled back under the covers and shut my eyes.

I flopped over onto my stomach—my favorite sleeping position. . . .

Crack!

The noise jerked me wide awake. It sounded like a tree being split by lightning.

Crack! There it was again.

The room was still dark, but I knew where the noise was coming from. The closet.

I crept slowly across the bed. My eyes locked on the closet door.

"No!" I cried as my eyes adjusted to the darkness. "This can't be!"

The door was bulging—bulging out into the room. The wood stretching and stretching—like a balloon about to pop.

Then I heard a *whooshing* sound. And the door seemed to suck itself back in.

Then it began to swell again. Pushing its way farther and farther into the room. The wood groaned and cracked. I could hear it splintering under the strain.

In and out.

In and out.

Every time the door swelled, the wood cracked some more.

The door was splitting open. Splitting right in two.

And then I spied it.

Jutting out through the split in the door.

A giant feeler.

8

"**H**elllp!" I screamed as I dived across my bed. I grabbed my glasses and shoved them on.

"Wes! Wes! What's wrong?" Mom stumbled into my room in her polka-dot nightgown and matching slippers.

She switched on the overhead light and sat down on my bed next to me. "Did you have a nightmare?" she asked, wrapping her arms around my shaking shoulders.

"No," I croaked. My tongue felt like cotton and I couldn't stop my teeth from chattering. "It's—

it's the m-m-mantis. He's trying to break out of the closet. He—"

Mom gave the closet a quick glance. "Slow down a minute, Wesley," she said, smoothing out my rumpled hair. "Take a deep breath and calm down."

I took a deep breath.

"Now, what did you say was in the closet?"

"The praying mantis. I tried to tell you at dinner," I said. "That's what was hidden in the Mystery Stereogram. You know, the one I got from Sal's Five-and-Ten?"

Mom gave a hesitant nod.

"Well, it's alive. And it can get out of the poster."

Mom rolled her eyes.

"You've got to believe me," I pleaded. "The mantis ate a moth that landed on the poster. And Fluffums."

"It ate Fluffums?" Mom exclaimed.

"No, no. The mantis pulled that clump of fur out of him. That's why I put the poster away in my closet. It's dangerous. It's really dangerous. And now the mantis almost smashed through the closet door."

Mom stared hard at the closet door again, then

44

peered around my room. My lamp lay on the floor with the shade knocked off. Pieces of the broken lightbulb were scattered everywhere. And my bedspread was stuffed under the closet door.

"I think we should open the closet and look inside, Wes," Mom said, patting my shoulder.

"I d-don't think that's a good idea, Mom," I stammered.

"Now, come on, Wes," she crooned. "We'll open up the closet door, and you'll see—everything will be fine. Just fine."

I forced myself over to the closet, tiptoeing around the pieces of broken glass. I examined the door closely. It seemed okay.

I rubbed my hand over the wood.

Smooth. No cracks. Not even a splinter.

Mom padded up beside me. "Now," she said patiently, "open the door."

I hesitated for a second. Yes, I decided. Mom was right. I had to open the closet. I had to know if the mantis was still waiting for me.

I slowly pulled the bedspread out from under the door.

My eyes were glued to the crack at the bottom.

No light. No dots. No buzzing sound. Safe so far.

Mom reached over my shoulder and turned the doorknob. A cold chill ran down my spine. Huge drops of perspiration dripped from my forehead. My pajamas began to stick to me.

"Hmmm. It seems to be stuck," Mom said. She twisted the doorknob both ways and pulled harder.

"No! Don't!" I shouted. I grabbed her wrist.

"Your hands are like ice cubes!" she exclaimed.

"I'm scared!" I admitted, gripping her arm tighter. "Maybe the mantis doesn't want us to get in. Maybe it's holding the door shut."

Mom gave me a quick hug. "It's okay," she said softly. "These old wooden doors just get sticky sometimes."

She tried the doorknob again. This time it turned.

My temples pounded. My pulse began to race. I held my breath as she slowly opened the door.

But I didn't look inside. I couldn't. I just studied her face. Waited for her reaction. But her expression didn't change.

She reached into the closet. Pulled on the chain that switches on the closet light. "Seems to be okay," she said. Then she stepped back so I could see inside.

My heart hammered in my chest as I pushed up my glasses to peer into the closet.

Everything seemed—normal.

Just as I'd left it.

The poster still lay behind the hula hoop—still tightly rolled up.

I shoved a couple of shirts aside. Nothing behind them.

I studied the lightbulb in the closet ceiling. Normal.

I felt the inside of the door. No cracks.

A sigh escaped my lips.

I shuffled over to my bed and collapsed into it. My arms and legs had turned to limp noodles. "Maybe it *was* a nightmare," I mumbled.

"They can feel awfully real," Mom answered. She picked up my lamp and returned it to the nightstand. "I'll be right back. I want to sweep up that broken glass before you cut your feet."

As soon as Mom left, I bolted over to the closet door and stuffed the bedspread back into the crack. This wasn't a dream. This was real. And I wasn't taking any chances.

When I heard Mom's slippers clomping back toward my room, I leaped back in bed. She handed me a new lightbulb, and I screwed it into my lamp right away. She didn't ask me about the bedspread—even though I know she noticed it shoved back under the door.

Mom swept the bulb pieces into a dustpan and emptied them into my wastebasket. "Should I switch this off, Wes?" She pointed to the overhead light.

"That's okay, Mom. I'll get it."

"Good night, Wes," she said. "Call me if you need me."

"Good night."

"Good night. What a joke, I thought. This was the worst night of my life. And it wasn't over yet.

I felt okay with Mom in the room. But as soon as she left, I couldn't stop staring at the closet. Waiting for something to happen. Something bad.

I thought maybe I should take the poster out to the garbage. But then I imagined the mantis escaping from the poster, bursting through the front door, and crawling up here to strangle me in my sleep.

No. Taking it outside wouldn't help.

I decided to bring the poster to school tomorrow and show it to Mr. Gosling. He's a scientist. Kind of. Maybe he'd have a logical explanation.

I left on all the lights. I propped the pillows

against the headboard so I could watch the closet. And just to be extra safe, I left my glasses on. Now I'd be ready to run if the dots came back.

Would they come floating out again?

Would they?

I vowed to stay up all night to find out.

9

Bzzzz. Bzzzz. Bzzzzz.

The dots are back!

I leaped out of bed and charged out of my room. I stood in the empty hallway, trying to catch my breath. My chest heaved up and down. I started to wheeze.

Bzzzzz. Bzzzzz. Bzzzzz.

Wait a minute. I knew that sound.

I stood up against the doorframe and peeked into my room.

No dots.

My alarm clock—ringing. Only my alarm.

I hurried back into my room and shut off the clock. Then I checked out my room.

The lights were still on.

My bedspread was still stuffed under the closet door.

I had made it through the night. Somehow.

I felt so relieved—until I realized I couldn't get dressed without opening the closet to get my clothes.

I crept over to the closet door and pressed my ear against it. No sounds. No insects buzzing.

I knelt and slid the bedspread out from under the crack. Then I opened the closet with a quick jerk.

No mantis!

I grabbed a pair of jeans and my red flannel shirt and pulled them on. I stuffed my feet into my socks and high-tops. Then I lifted the poster with two fingers. The paper felt damp and sort of sticky. I slid it into my backpack and raced downstairs.

I couldn't wait to talk to Mr. Gosling. He knew all about optics. He had a scientist's mind. He'd help me figure this out.

"You okay this morning?" Dad asked. He began slicing a banana over his cornflakes.

"Uh—sure," I answered. I shook some cereal into a bowl and splashed on some milk. "Just a bad dream," I added. I didn't want to talk to my parents about the mantis again until I figured out what was going on.

I wolfed down the cereal and chugged a glass of apple juice. "Got to go," I called. I slipped my backpack on and headed for the door.

Clawd wound himself around my legs. I bent over to pet him, and the poster started to slide out of my backpack. "Yeooww!" Clawd tore away from me like a streak of lightning.

I sighed. "Bye," I called again and left. I had to get some answers today.

As I walked to school, I kept reaching back and touching the poster. Making sure it was still there. I felt as if I had some sort of monster trapped in a bottle. And I didn't want it to get loose.

I felt extra glad when I spotted Lauren waiting for me at our usual corner. She was wearing a bright blue jacket that matched her eyes. And she had her black hair pulled back with a matching headband.

Lauren frowned as I jogged up to her. "Hey, Wes, you look wrecked. Are you okay?"

"Not really," I admitted. I reached back and touched the poster again.

We turned onto Hawthorne Street, and I told Lauren about everything. The mantis. The moth. Clawd, Fluffums, the real, live nightmare in my bedroom last night. And my plan to ask Mr. Gosling for help. I talked nonstop.

When I finally finished, we were a block away from school. "Well, what do you think?"

"Uh," Lauren started. She chewed her lip for a minute. "Wes, this isn't a joke or anything, is it?" she asked. "I mean, is this a story you're just trying out on me? Before you tell it to the twins?"

"Of course not!" I protested. "I wouldn't joke about something like this. It's too weird. Besides, why would I try to fool you?"

"Okay, okay." Lauren held her hand up. "But you have to admit—it is a really strange story."

"I know. But you *do* believe me, don't you?"

"Sure," Lauren said. But I could tell she really wasn't sure. "Talking to Mr. Gosling is a good idea," Lauren continued. "He's logical and all. Maybe he can figure it out. Anyway, whatever happens, Wes, remember—you beat the twins!"

"Yeah. I did. I almost forgot." We laughed and slapped each other a high five.

Then Lauren's face turned serious. "You know—maybe that creepy guy in the five-and-ten was right. Remember, he kept saying, 'You have the power to see.' Maybe it has something to do with that."

Lauren was really starting to believe me!

We crossed the street. A lot of kids were already hanging around outside the school.

"Hey, there's Kim." Lauren pointed to a red-haired girl wearing bright green leggings and a matching jacket. "I have to borrow her history notes. See you later," she called as she ran ahead. "And be careful!"

"See you later," I called, turning up the cobblestone walkway alone.

I reached back one more time to touch the poster—and something yanked me hard from behind. I stumbled backward.

I tried to turn. But it held both my arms in a tight grip.

I tried to scream. But no words came out.

I struggled to escape, but the more I twisted, the tighter it clung to me. Tighter, tighter. Hauling me right off the sidewalk.

I felt something sharp dig into my neck. Something sharp—like pincers.

10

"**H**elp!" The word exploded from my throat. "Somebody help me!" I twisted and fought to get free.

And then the thing released me.

I thudded to the ground—and spun around.

The "thing" had four arms. And four legs. And tails growing out of the sides of two ugly snorting heads.

Corny and Gabby.

I sighed and pushed myself to my feet. I felt like a total jerk.

They stared at me, giggling and snorting. "Got you, huh?" Corny taunted.

"Yeah," I shot out. "You're a riot. A real riot. Corny."

"Don't call me that!" Corny scowled.

"Yeah, don't call her that," Gabby echoed, twirling her ponytail.

"Your family owes our family money," Corny announced. "Money for the vet bills our parents had to pay." She narrowed her eyes.

"Lots of money." Gabby sneered.

"And that's not all," Corny jumped in. "The police are going to take your vicious cat away, too."

I could feel my face grow red-hot. I wanted to lunge for the twins and yank them around by their stupid ponytails. "No way! *Your* dog ran into *our* house," I insisted.

At least I beat them at the contest, I thought. And the second my prize arrives, I will rub it in their faces. I will never let them live it down.

But for now I would have to follow Lauren's advice—and ignore them.

Without another word I adjusted my backpack, turned, and left.

* * *

I met Lauren at the lockers right before science. I'd gotten through the first couple of hours of school with no problems. I told her what the twins said that morning about the police taking Clawd away.

"They're making it up. They're such jerks," she said, slamming her locker shut with an extra-loud bang.

I shoved my math book into my locker and hung my jacket on the hook. Then, very carefully, I inched the poster out of my backpack. "I'm going to try and catch Mr. Gosling before class starts."

"Good idea," Lauren agreed.

I turned to go—and a hand reached out from nowhere and snatched my glasses off.

I spun around and dropped the poster. It unrolled on the floor.

"Hey! I can't see!" I yelled. "Give me my glasses back!"

The twins! Those jerks! They had my glasses. They always steal my glasses. They know I can't see without them.

I can't wait to teach those twins a lesson, I fumed.

I heard the twins snorting and giggling all the way up the stairs. They were in Mr. Gosling's

58

class, too. I'd get my glasses back then. But first, I had to find Mr. Gosling.

"Come on, Wes," Lauren interrupted my thoughts. "The bell's about to ring."

I squatted down next to the poster. I wanted to roll it up right away. It felt safer that way.

I tried not to peer directly at the poster. It still scared me—a lot. Instead, I glanced at the tile floor next to the poster. But my eyes were drawn to the colored dots as I rolled it up.

I glanced at it for only a second. But that's all it took.

There it stood.

The mantis.

Staring back at me—with its huge, wet, shiny eyes.

I jumped back in horror and screamed, "It's back! It's back!" I couldn't stop screaming. "It's back!"

"Wes! Wes! What's wrong?" Lauren cried.

I couldn't answer. I could only stare. Stare at the mantis as it fought its way out of the poster.

It twisted and strained, like a prehistoric monster trapped in a tar pit. And all the time it watched me. Watched me with those terrifying bug eyes.

Do something. Do something! a voice cried out inside me. But my feet froze to the floor.

I heard Lauren yelling. But she sounded so far away. I was in some kind of trance. The blood pounded in my temples. My heart felt about to burst out of my chest.

DO SOMETHING! the voice screamed in my head.

I grabbed the poster.

My fingers fumbled as I began to roll it up.

I could feel the mantis pushing, pushing against my curled fingers.

I kept rolling up the poster. Faster. Faster.

And then I lost my grip—and the poster sprang open.

"Ahhh!" I yelled as two long back feelers lunged out and dug into my hands.

I dropped the poster.

The feelers waved wildly in the air as it fell. I slammed my foot down to smash them—and missed. The mantis buzzed furiously.

I stomped again. Harder.

One of its long, spindly legs rose out of the poster. And its razor-sharp pincer locked around my ankle.

"Ow!" I howled, shaking my leg wildly. "It's got me! It's got me!"

"What's happening?" Lauren cried. "What's got you?"

She couldn't see it! The mantis had exploded right out of the poster. It was huge! And she still couldn't see it.

It quivered and shook as it freed itself from the paper.

And it began to grow larger. Much larger than the size of the poster!

"Lauren," I gasped. "It's the mantis. It's out of the poster! It's attacking me! And it's huge!"

The mantis reared up on its back legs. It shot out a pincer and gripped my wrist. And squeezed. Squeezed until my hand felt numb. Squeezed until my fingers turned purple.

I clawed at the pincer, trying to tear it off me.

The mantis's legs lashed out. The sharp barbs tore at my shirt. Ripped right through it. My body stung and burned as its pincers pierced my skin.

It continued to grow. Up. Up.

Now it stood as tall as me!

Its enormous, ugly bug face stared into my eyes.

Then its feelers shot through my hair.

"Get it off me!" I screamed again and again.

My arms and legs flailed madly as I tried to struggle free. The mantis wrapped its strong, spindly arms around my neck.

Was it trying to choke me?

Where was Lauren? Why wasn't she helping? "Laur—" Her name stuck in my throat as I gasped for air.

I jerked my head up to try to loosen the huge insect's deadly grip.

"Lauren? Where are you?" I choked out.

"Lauren? Lauren?"

"Lauren?"

I saw her. Hurrying down the hall.

Leaving me to fight the giant mantis!

"Aaaagggghhh." A gurgling sound escaped my throat as the mantis squeezed tighter. I couldn't breathe. Bursts of color exploded before my eyes.

I flung my head back.

I stumbled through the hall with the mantis clutching my throat.

Then I whirled around and slammed the mantis into the row of lockers. I heard that high-pitched buzz again, and I felt the pincers loosen.

The insect opened its huge jaws. I could see deep into its mouth. I could smell its sour breath. It snapped its jaws shut inches from my face.

I shoved one arm between the creature and my chest and hurled it from my body. It crashed to the floor with a horrible screech.

Then I spotted Lauren. Leaning against the lockers with her arms folded.

"Very convincing, Wes." She smiled. "If I didn't know better, I'd swear you were wrestling with a huge, invisible praying mantis."

She reached out her hand and gave me a playful shove. "We're going to be really late if—"

The mantis lashed out and locked a pincer around Lauren's wrist.

"Owww! Wes!" she screamed. "Something's got me! Get it off!"

I took a deep breath and gave a sort of karate chop to the mantis's long front leg.

The mantis cried out and flew across the hallway.

"W-what happened?" Lauren stammered, rubbing the red, raw spot where the mantis had sunk its pincer.

"The mantis," I whispered. I watched as its big head slowly turned and its enormous eyes scanned the empty hall. "It's still here, but it's not looking at us right now. Wait. I think it sees something down the hall."

I squinted, but I couldn't see very well—things were a total blur without my glasses.

"It's Mr. Gosling!" Lauren cried. "Quick, Wes! Stop him and tell him about the mantis."

Lauren couldn't see the mantis. But at least she really truly believed me now.

Mr. Gosling ambled down the hall balancing a high pile of books under his chin.

He headed straight for us.

And the mantis.

"Look out!" I yelled.

Too late.

The mantis seized his ankle and sank its jaw into it.

Mr. Gosling let out a low moan. His long legs buckled underneath him. He tumbled face-first on the floor and slid down the hall on his stomach. Dragging the mantis behind him.

I snatched up one of the books he dropped— *Fun with Insects.* I stuck it in my back pocket. It might come in handy, I thought.

I grabbed another book and hurled it at the mantis.

Missed!

"Wes, what are you doing?" Lauren whispered.

"Trying to hit the mantis," I said.

I heaved another book at it.

"Darn! Missed again."

"Where is it, Wes?" Lauren asked. "What's it doing?"

I squinted down the hall. Mr. Gosling climbed to his feet. "It had Mr. Gosling by the ankle," I answered. "Now it's lying right behind him."

"I'd like an explanation," Mr. Gosling bellowed as he strode toward us. His baggy gray cardigan flapped behind him. "Why are you throwing those books? And who tripped me?"

I knew this wasn't the time to get Mr. Gosling's theories about the poster. I had to talk fast. "Uh. No one tripped you. At least Lauren and I didn't trip you. But I did throw your books. I'm sorry about that. But I had to—"

"Had to throw books?" Mr. Gosling questioned me, staring over his glasses. "We'll deal with this later. Now, please help me pick them up." He bent over and started gathering his books.

Lauren and I helped. I kept one eye on the mantis the whole time.

"Quick, Lauren," I whispered. "It's coming!"

"Run for it!" she screamed, dropping her pile of books and sprinting down the hall.

Mr. Gosling pushed himself to his feet and patted his tie down. "What is wrong with her? She threw my books on the floor. I really don't understand this behavior. Maybe you'd both better come with me for a serious talk."

"No, please, Mr. Gosling," I begged. "There's a logical explanation for all this. I'm sure there is. But I need you to help me figure it out."

"Figure it out?" Mr. Gosling asked. "You want me to figure out why *you* are misbehaving?"

"Where is it? Is it gone?" Lauren yelled from halfway down the hall, her voice high and squeaky.

"No," I called.

I studied the mantis, trying to decide what it would do next. It had stopped crawling. Now it seemed to be waiting. Almost motionless. Then, very slowly, it rubbed one of its pincers on the top of its head.

Then it took a step toward Mr. Gosling.

"It's getting closer," I warned.

"What's getting closer?" Mr. Gosling demanded.

I swallowed hard.

"Tell him!" Lauren urged. "Tell him before it's too late!"

"Too late for what?" he asked. "Class?" He sounded more confused than angry now.

"Um. Yes. Class," I answered. "Let's go." I scooped up the books Lauren had dropped. I grabbed Mr. Gosling's elbow and quickly steered him around the mantis and over to the stairs.

Lauren started to climb up first.

"Wait!" I yelled. "Where's the poster? I have to have the poster!"

"There!" Lauren pointed. "Near the lockers."

I ran down the hall and scooped it off the floor. As I rolled it up, I noticed a large blank space. The space where the mantis had been.

Lauren raced down the hall, tugging my arm. "Come on," she urged, searching the hall for some sign of the creature. "Where is the thing?"

"It's okay," I answered. "It's busy."

Mr. Gosling stood by the staircase rearranging the books in his arms. The mantis crouched nearby. But it wasn't paying any attention to him. It held its two front legs together in front of its huge eyes.

"Busy doing what?" Lauren asked. I could tell she was working to stay calm.

68

"It's behind Mr. Gosling. Don't worry, it doesn't seem interested in him. It looks as if it's praying or something," I whispered.

Lauren wrenched my arm. "Doesn't that mean it's getting ready to attack?"

12

Yes!

Lauren was right!

Now I remembered. The mantis had raised its legs in a praying position right before it ate the moth!

"Let's get out of here!" I shouted.

The mantis began rocking back and forth, with its front legs pressed together.

We raced over to Mr. Gosling. I grabbed for his sleeve, yanking him up the steps.

"Be careful, Wes," he warned. "I'm going to

drop these books again. It doesn't matter if we're a few minutes late."

"Don't want to be any later than we already are," I replied.

"That's right," Lauren agreed.

I heard that terrible buzzing sound—like a million angry mosquitoes. Lauren didn't seem to hear it at all. I glanced over my shoulder.

"It's still behind us," I whispered to Lauren as we reached the top of the stairs. "It's crawling up. Following us!"

"Tell him!" she urged.

We had almost reached the science lab. I jumped in front of the door, blocking it. "Mr. Gosling, there's something you have to know. It's about the stereogram. The one the twins brought to class. There's a mantis in it. A praying mantis. And it's not just 3-D. It's actually alive—"

Mr. Gosling pushed past me. "After class," he answered. I could tell he was fed up.

Lauren and I hurried to our seats. She sits in the back of the class. I sit near the front, right next to the twins.

"Give me back my glasses," I ordered them.

"What glasses?" Corny asked.

71

"Yeah, what glasses?" Gabby chimed in.

"My glasses, you—"

I heard a horrible scraping sound at the door. It opened a crack and two long black feelers poked inside. They waved back and forth—searching the air. Searching for something.

"Oh, no!" I moaned.

I turned to Lauren. "It's here!" I mouthed.

"Is there something you would like to share with the rest of the class, Wes?" Mr. Gosling asked.

"Umm, I really need to talk to you about the 3-D poster." I glanced at the door. It swung open wider. The mantis's huge head appeared. Its jaws dripped saliva. "Someone might get hurt if—"

"I told you—we will talk about the poster after class," Mr. Gosling said sternly. Then he began to make his way over to the door.

I wanted to cover my eyes with my hands. Or disappear under my desk. But I knew I had to warn Mr. Gosling. I jumped up from my seat—but I wasn't fast enough.

Mr. Gosling reached the door and—shut it hard, smashing one of the mantis's back legs.

Phew. That was a close one.

The mantis's leg re-formed itself. The buzzing

grew louder than ever. I could feel it vibrating through my body. My ears pounded. I covered them with my hands, trying to block out the hideous noise.

"But after class will be too late—" I tried to warn Mr. Gosling.

"After class!" Mr. Gosling exclaimed. "And please don't cover your ears when I'm speaking to you."

The twins started to snort.

I thought my eardrums were going to explode.

"Yes!" I shouted. "I hear you."

"Why are you shouting? What's wrong with you today, Wes?" Mr. Gosling asked. "Are you sick?"

"No," I muttered. I wished I could tell him yes. Then he would send me down to the nurse. The nurse would call my mom. And my mom would come and take me home.

But it was too late for that.

I bought the poster.

I ignored Sal's warnings.

And now I was the only one who could see the mantis. I was the only one who could hear the buzzing. So I had to stay. I had to stop the mantis. If I could.

73

"Let's continue our study of the eye," Mr. Gosling started.

The buzzing slowly faded, but the mantis remained perched by the door. Mr. Gosling began pacing back and forth in front of the classroom—the way he always does. His hands shoved deep into his pockets.

The mantis crept up behind him and followed him—back and forth across the room. Back and forth. It paused when Mr. Gosling paused. It turned when Mr. Gosling turned.

I wanted to scream.

At least it's not praying, I thought. But the mantis definitely had its eye on Mr. Gosling.

Mr. Gosling turned to the chalkboard and drew a side view of the human eye. The mantis reached out to take a swipe at him.

It missed.

I let out a loud gasp.

Mr. Gosling glared at me. Then he turned back to his drawing.

The mantis tried again.

This time its pincer hit the chalkboard.

Screeeech.

Everybody cried out. A few kids held their

74

hands over their ears. Mr. Gosling glared at me again. As if it were my fault!

At first I was surprised that everyone could hear the *screech*. Then I remembered that other people couldn't see the mantis or hear it buzzing—but they could feel it grab them. So I guess it made sense that they could hear its pincer scraping the chalkboard.

Mr. Gosling slammed the chalk in the rack and marched over to a corner of the room—where his favorite specimen stood under a white sheet.

"Okay," he announced, whipping the sheet off. A human skeleton hung from a stand. It was a little shorter than Mr. Gosling. "We're going to examine the skull today."

The mantis inched over to the skeleton. Its feelers were waving all over the place. It tilted its enormous head, staring hard at the bones. Saliva dripped from it jaws and puddled at its feet. It was hungry, I realized.

I was so nervous, I fumbled with my ruler and it crashed to the floor.

Mr. Gosling ignored me. He rolled the skeleton closer to the class. "Have a look at the bones around your eyes."

"Ooh, gross!" Gabby cried.

Everybody laughed.

The mantis leaned forward and seemed to be sniffing the skeleton. I leaned forward, too. My stomach heaved.

The mantis caught the skeleton's hand between its gaping jaws. It started chewing the finger bones.

The whole class gasped. "Cool trick!" someone yelled.

"I think it's hungry," I mouthed to Lauren.

Mr. Gosling stared at the arm. It looked as if it were waving to us.

"Who's doing that?" Mr. Gosling demanded. "Wes?"

"No!" I protested. "But you have to listen to me. I think it's *really* dangerous now. I think it's hungry."

"What's hungry?" Gabby asked. "The skeleton?"

A few kids laughed.

"It sure looks thin," Corny added.

More laughter.

The mantis grabbed one of the skeleton's legs and started gnawing on the knee.

"What's it doing now?" Gabby called.

"I think it's the cancan," Corny cracked.

The class went completely out of control. They thought the whole thing was a big joke.

Mr. Gosling grabbed the stand and wheeled the skeleton away from the mantis. "This is not a toy," he declared. "I want an apology from the person responsible."

The room fell silent. Except for the sounds coming from the mantis—buzzing and snapping its pincers recklessly in the air. "Don't move the skeleton!" I cried. "You're making it angry!"

The class exploded into laughter.

Mr. Gosling strode over to my desk. He glared down at me. "If I hear one more outburst, you are out of here. Do you understand that?" he growled. "And I don't mean detention. I mean suspension. From school!"

What could I say?

I felt so helpless. I needed to explain everything to Mr. Gosling. To get him on my side.

I placed my head in my hands. Think, Wes. Think.

Then I jerked my head up. Where was the mantis? I'd lost track of him.

Oh, no! I slid down in my seat.

The creature had discovered the corner in the back of the room where we kept the class animals.

I thought of the moth.

I remembered Fluffums and the clump of hair.

And I watched in horror as the creature reached its pincer out to the hamster cage.

13

I stared in horror as it pulled the bars of the hamster cage apart.

I closed my eyes for a moment. Trying to come up with a plan. But a terrifying picture crowded my mind. I saw the mantis shove the hamster into its waiting, dripping jaws—and swallowing it whole. I imagined it moving on to the guinea pigs, the white mice, and the baby frogs.

Here goes, I thought. I'll probably be expelled from school—but I had to take action.

I climbed up on my lab stool. "Free the animals!" I shouted to Lauren. At least that way maybe they wouldn't be sitting targets. Maybe they could run and hide.

Lauren jumped up and ran to the frog aquarium. She scooped up the frogs, two and three at a time, and plunked them on the floor.

They sat there frozen.

The mantis plodded toward them.

They slowly lifted their little heads in the air. They seemed to be sniffing. Then they started hopping in all directions.

Some of the kids began to scream and climb on top of their desks. Most of the kids were laughing.

"Stop that this instant!" I could barely make out Mr. Gosling's voice above the noise.

Lauren ignored him and moved on to the next cage.

"Free them all!" I shouted. I ran to the chalkboard and grabbed the wooden pointer.

"What do you think you're doing?" Mr. Gosling demanded. He grabbed my shoulder and shook it hard.

"Look out!" I yelled as I broke free from his grasp. I charged over to the animal cages, waving the pointer like a sword.

The mantis stood over a cage full of fat white mice. Drooling and praying.

Rocking back and forth.

The mice squeaked wildly, jumping up and down like pieces of popping popcorn.

I made my way carefully to the mantis. The pointer kept slipping from my sweaty palm. I crept up behind the creature and jabbed its side. It spun around and yanked the stick right out of my hand—but it backed off a few feet, buzzing furiously.

I knocked the mice cage over and urged the mice out.

"What are you doing with those mice?" Mr. Gosling exclaimed, throwing his hands up in the air.

"I'm saving their lives!" I answered, clapping loudly so they would scatter.

"What about the turtles?" Jimmy Peterson called out. Everyone was getting into it now.

"Let them go, too!" I commanded. And he did.

The turtles wouldn't move—no matter how much anyone yelled at them. A few kids picked them up so they wouldn't get squashed.

Someone let the garter snake go. The mantis lunged for it. But the snake wriggled under the radiator in a flash. The mantis sent a pincer out, but it couldn't reach.

81

"Good!" I shouted. Now I turned to the bat's cage.

"Not my bat!" Mr. Gosling pleaded, clutching his chest.

The bat was Mr. Gosling's favorite class pet. He found it on a hiking trip. Its wing was broken and Mr. Gosling nursed it back to health. Mr. Gosling would want me to set the bat free if he could see the mantis, I convinced myself.

I flung the black cover off the cage and pulled open the door. The mantis lumbered in our direction. The bat didn't move. It hung from its branch, all wrapped up in its wings.

"It's asleep!" I yelled to Lauren. "And the mantis is headed right for it!"

"Tickle it!" she called.

I brushed it lightly on its underside with my finger. That did it. The bat woke up and burst through the door, excited to be free.

"Get him! Get him!" Mr. Gosling yelled, chasing after the bat.

Someone opened the door to let the mice out, and the bat escaped into the hallway.

Mr. Gosling ran out the door and slammed it behind him.

Suddenly the classroom went quiet. The kids

stopped shouting. All the animals had found hiding places.

It felt creepy.

"Where is it now?" Lauren whispered.

"It's n-not near us," I stammered. "It's poking around Corny's desk."

"Hey! Who knocked my microscope over?" Corny whined. She hurried back to her desk. Gabby was right behind her. But the mantis was no longer there. It had moved on.

What would it do next? I wondered.

"Ooh, my notes are all wet," Gabby complained. "And slimy." She picked them up by the corner.

"Mantis drool," I whispered to Lauren.

"Where is it now?" she asked.

"It's—it's coming this way."

I spotted the pointer on the floor. I snatched it up and crouched under one of the lab tables. My knees trembled and my hands shook.

"What are you going to do?" Lauren asked. She crouched beside me.

"I'm—I'm going to try to stab it with the pointer," I said, inching toward the mantis. I could see its thin green legs as it wobbled down one row and up another.

My pulse started to race as it crawled closer and

83

closer. A few more feet—and I'd be able to reach it.

Then the bell rang.

"Lunch!" someone shouted.

The kids gathered up their stuff and stampeded out the door. The mantis joined the crowd.

"Where is it now?" Lauren demanded.

"It's—it's gone," I answered.

"Great!" Lauren cheered.

"There's just one problem." I sighed.

"What?" Lauren asked.

"It's headed for the cafeteria."

14

"**D**on't go!" Lauren shouted as I ran out the classroom door. "Don't go without this!" She waved the poster in the air.

I grabbed it. Then we scrambled down the stairs and raced to the cafeteria. Just as we reached the entrance, Lauren skidded to a stop and seized my arm. "What's that noise?"

We both listened.

My stomach churned. "Screaming."

We raced inside. I was certain the mantis had attacked someone.

An apple whizzed by my head.

"Food fight!" someone shrieked.

Food fight? They were screaming about a food fight?

My eyes darted around the cafeteria, searching for the creature. "I see it," I whispered to Lauren. "It's wandering from table to table. And it's drooling like crazy."

"Who took my Twinkie?" a skinny, freckle-faced kid shouted.

"Who stole my peanut-butter-and-banana sandwich?" another kid yelled.

I watched the mantis grab a tub of cottage cheese and scoop up a big glob with its pincer. No one even noticed the tub hovering in the air. There was too much food flying around.

The mantis shoved a ball of the cottage cheese in its mouth—and spit it right back out. It flicked a chunk of it right into the lunchroom teacher's gray hair. Then it began to whip its pincer back and forth with fury, spattering white dots of cottage cheese everywhere.

"Yuck! Who's throwing this stuff?" a kid in a Dodgers baseball cap complained. "It's disgusting." He scraped it off his blue shirt and slung it at someone else.

"Is the mantis doing all this?" Lauren asked.

"Most of it," I answered. "I can't see too well. Corny still has my glasses." I can't wait till I get my hands on her, I muttered to myself.

"What is it doing right now?" she asked.

"It's weird, Lauren," I said as I squinted at it. "Its snatching food and sniffing it—and flinging it away. It isn't eating anything."

"Maybe it's not hungry," Lauren replied.

I shook my head. "It's hungry all right. It's dripping pools of drool. I just don't get it."

Suddenly I remembered the *Fun with Insects* book. I yanked it out of my back pocket. I flipped to the praying mantis page.

"Uh-oh," I moaned.

Lauren tried to read over my shoulder. "What, Wes? What?"

I took a deep breath. "According to this book, the mantis prefers its food alive."

"Alive?" Lauren's huge blue eyes grew wide. "As in walking, breathing alive?"

"Uh-huh."

PLOP. A big glob of carrots landed on my sneaker. Well, at least it doesn't have a cow eye in it, I thought as we both stared down at it—the way the carrots did yesterday. I wished that day had never happened. Because that was the day I first saw the twins' Mystery Stereogram.

Why couldn't I see the mantis that day? I wondered. How come I could see it now? What was different? What—

"What's it doing now? What's it doing now?" Lauren interrupted my thoughts.

I searched the room. It was way in the back of the cafeteria. At that distance I couldn't see it at all.

CRASH!

A huge crash from the back. Followed by a long, terrifying scream.

"What's happening, Lauren? I can't see!"

"A table flipped over by itself!" Lauren yelled.

"I doubt it." We raced to the back of the cafeteria.

I really wish I had my glasses, I thought. "My glasses! That's it!" I shouted.

"What's going on?" Lauren asked the kids gathered around the upside-down table.

"Cornelia is trapped under there," a girl in a bright purple T-shirt answered.

"Yeah," Chad Miller added. "I tried to pull it off

88

her—but something cut me." He held up his hand. A deep jagged scratch ran across the back. "I couldn't see what it was. It was like—invisible or something." Chad shook his head, confused.

Lauren and I pushed through the crowd of kids—and there was Corny. Her legs were pinned under part of the table. But that wasn't what was holding her down. The mantis was draped across her chest!

Her hands thrashed the air as she screamed, "Get it off me!"

"Lauren! It's sitting on Corny. I have to get my glasses from her!"

"I know she's a total jerk. But shouldn't we help her before we worry about the glasses?" Lauren protested.

"No! I mean yes . . . I mean . . . the first time I saw the poster, I had my glasses on and everything was okay," I quickly explained. "But when I look at it without my glasses . . . I make it come alive. I think."

I stared down at Corny to check the mantis. A long strand of drool stretched from its mouth to the floor. And it was rubbing its front legs together—praying.

I shoved some kids aside and knelt next to Corny. The mantis started to rock back and forth.

"Give me my glasses," I ordered.

"First get me out of here," Corny screeched. "Something's on top of me! But I can't see it!"

I stared at her hard. "If you want to get out of here alive, give me my glasses. Now!"

Corny's face grew pale. The mantis was rocking. Rocking back and forth. Corny's eyes darted frantically to see what was pressing against her.

The mantis raised its pincers.

It opened its huge, gaping jaw.

A thick wad of drool oozed out on Corny's arm.

Corny screamed.

"Now!" I yelled at her. "Now!"

"Here!" She slid my glasses out of her pocket.

I leaped up and shoved them on. I had only seconds before the mantis would strike.

I concentrated on the mantis.

Nothing happened.

"Is it working, Wes?" Lauren whispered.

"Ssh," I said. "I have to concentrate." Beads of sweat dripped down my face as I focused.

The mantis moved slightly. It was crouching.

Getting ready to spring.

To lunge for Corny's neck.

I stared as hard as I could.

My head ached.

My eyes throbbed and burned.

I wanted to close them. I needed to close them.

My eyelids started to drop—and then it happened.

Tiny dots began to appear. Hundreds of them. Thousands of them. Orange, green, pink, and yellow. Fluorescent dots all over the mantis's body.

They began to glow. Brighter and brighter.

Don't blink. Don't blink, I chanted to myself.

The dots began to swarm. They swirled and raced up and down the mantis's legs. All the way up its body. Up to its feelers. Up to its head.

Then the dots whirled apart. It was like watching an explosion in slow motion.

The dots flooded the cafeteria. Bouncing off the tables. The chairs. The kids. Buzzing. Buzzing.

And then they were gone.

Corny wiggled out from under the table. "Thanks for nothing, Wes," she muttered.

"Did it work?" Lauren asked softly.

I unrolled the poster clutched in my hand.

The blank space was—gone.

I breathed out the longest sigh of my life.

"It's back in the poster, Lauren."

"Yes! You were right!" she cried. "We're safe!"

"Not yet," I corrected her. "We're not safe until we destroy this poster for good."

15

"**T**he scissors are in the top drawer, next to the refrigerator," I told Lauren. We had a long talk when we got home from school about the best way to get rid of the mantis. This was all we could think of.

"Are you sure it's safe?" Lauren asked.

"I hope so," I said.

I read a note stuck to the refrigerator. "Mom says she and Dad took Vicky shopping. So this is the best time."

I made certain my glasses were firmly in place. Then I rolled the poster out on the kitchen table.

Lauren handed me the scissors.

I laughed nervously. "My hands are shaking."

I swallowed hard. "Here goes." I turned the poster from side to side, trying to decide where to cut. Actually I was stalling. I didn't know what would happen if I cut the poster. Would the mantis burst out if I sliced through the dots?

I squeezed my eyes shut and snipped into the paper. I did it really quickly. I was scared.

No buzzing.

I opened my eyes and snipped again. This time I cut the poster in half.

"Think it worked?" Lauren asked.

I stared down at the two pieces. "I don't know."

"Are you going to make sure?" she asked.

I nodded. "I guess I have to."

"Be careful. Have your glasses ready," Lauren warned.

My stomach clenched. "I will." I slid my glasses down my nose. Then I peeked over the top of them at the left half of the poster.

I jerked my head away and shoved my glasses up. "It's still there," I groaned.

"Okay, okay," Lauren said. "Let's stay calm." But she didn't sound calm. "Maybe we just need to cut it in smaller pieces."

Lauren picked up the scissors. "I'll do it this time." She made a tiny cut, then glanced over at me. "Turn around, okay? It makes me nervous when you stare at the poster—even with your glasses on."

I turned away from the kitchen table.

Snip. Snip. Snip. I grew more and more nervous with each little snip.

I heard Lauren slam the scissors down on the table. Then I heard a tearing sound.

"What are you doing?" I asked.

"I'm ripping it up. It's quicker than the scissors," she explained.

Riiiip. I hated that sound even more than the scissor snips. A drop of sweat rolled down my cheek. I wiped my clammy hands on my jeans.

I heard Lauren rip the paper again and again and again.

What if it's still there?

What if we're only making things worse?

What if we're making the mantis *angry?*

"That ought to do it," she announced. "You can turn around now."

I whirled to face her—and gasped. A mound of paper filled the center of the table. Tiny pieces about the size of the fingernail on my pinky.

Lauren's face flushed pink. "I didn't want to take any chances."

"I guess I should check it again," I said. I hoped she would say I didn't have to.

But she nodded. I knew she was right. We had to be sure the creature was really gone.

I pulled my glasses down to the end of my nose. The pieces were so tiny. I could barely see them.

I leaned over the table.

I still couldn't be sure.

A drop of sweat ran down my chin and plopped onto the pile.

I bent my head lower and lower. Closer and closer.

The blood pounded in my ears.

"Be careful not to—"

Before Lauren could finish her warning, it was too late.

A tiny pincer lashed out at my face.

My glasses went flying.

I heard them hit the floor.

"Lauren! Get my glasses!" I yelled.

"Where did they go?" she cried, searching the floor on her hands and knees.

"I don't know!" I answered. "Hurry!"

Tiny legs burst out of each piece of the poster.
Tiny eyes glared up at me.
Sharp little pincers clicked open and shut.
They swarmed over the table.
Hundreds.
Hundreds of miniature praying mantises!

16

"They're back!"

"Huh? They?" Lauren shrieked.

"They're pouring out of all the pieces!" I cried.

"Oh, no!" Lauren moaned. "What do we do now?"

"We've got to find my glasses!"

"I'm checking under the table," she called.

"Wait!" I yelled. But it was too late.

The mantises marched down the table legs—toward Lauren. The kitchen filled with their horrible buzzing.

I grabbed a dish towel from the counter and whipped it at the little monsters.

"Get out of there! The mantises are headed right for you!"

Lauren scrambled out from under the table. "They're on me! They're on me!" she cried, jumping up and down. "I think they're in my hair!" She leaned forward and slapped at her head.

"Hold still!" I yelled at her. "Let me look!" The buzzing grew louder and louder. I could hardly think.

She shook her head violently. "I can't hold still, Wes. I just can't! Do something! Please!"

I grabbed her head to hold it still. The green insects swarmed over her hair—burrowing deeper and deeper.

I tried to pick them out, but it was impossible. They lashed out with their sharp pincers. "Quick! Go to the sink!"

"Water!" Lauren shouted. "Perfect. We'll drown them."

Then I turned on the cold tap full force and guided Lauren's head under it.

I turned to check the table. "Oh, no!" I spotted a mantis launch off the table and soar into the air. "They can fly."

"It's not working," Lauren called from the sink. "I can feel them. They're starting to bite!"

"No, it is working, Lauren," I said, peering at her head. "I can see them spilling off."

I felt a sharp sting on the back of my neck. Then on my forehead. My nose. One of my ears.

The mantises swarmed around my head.

Dodged at my face.

Clawed into my skin.

I stumbled backward, pawing frantically at my head.

Then I heard a terrifying sound.

And I knew we were doomed.

17

CRUNNCH.

I heard a crunch. Underfoot.

And I knew what I had stepped on. With a sinking feeling I snatched my glasses up from the floor. Maybe only one lens broke, I silently wished. Maybe only one.

Nope.

Both of them—smashed.

Yes. We're both doomed, I thought.

I grabbed the dish towel again. This time I threw it over my head, trying to protect myself from the stinging creatures.

Think, Wes. Think, I ordered myself. They are bugs. How do you get rid of bugs?

I dashed to the wall switch and flicked on the ceiling light.

Yes! The mantises flew toward the light and began to circle. A few bounced off the bulb and dropped to the table. Then they staggered up and launched themselves at the glowing bulb again.

They were under control. For now.

Lauren pulled her head out from under the tap. Water streamed down her long hair. Down her face. "Where are they?"

I pointed to the ceiling light.

Lauren grinned. "Great! Now all we have to do is find your glasses!"

"Uh. I already did," I admitted. I held them up.

"Oh, no! Now what do we do?" Lauren wailed. "Do you have an extra pair?"

"That *was* my extra pair," I answered.

I peered up at the insects, squinting into the light. The buzzing noise suddenly changed to a low humming sound.

My eyes felt itchy, but I kept staring—because I noticed a small change.

"Something's happening," I murmured.

"What?" Lauren grabbed my arm. "What's happening. Tell me!"

"They're changing."

"Changing? How?" Lauren demanded. "They're not growing, are they? Please, don't tell me they're growing."

"No. They're definitely not growing. But they're not getting smaller, either." I blinked several times. "They're turning into those dots. It's just like what happened in the cafeteria!"

"Yes!" Lauren cried. "That means they're disappearing!"

"I don't think so, Lauren."

"Well, what are they doing?" she cried.

"They're still up there. Humming. Orange, pink, yellow, and green humming dots," I explained. "Now they're swirling around the light. Really fast. The colors are almost melting together."

"Maybe they're dying," Lauren suggested.

"No!" I exclaimed. "No! They're forming one big ball of color now! One big ball of green!"

"Oh, n-noooo," Lauren wailed. "Look!"

I ripped my eyes away from the swirling green ball of color.

"Look!" Lauren cried again, pointing to the table with a trembling hand. "The poster," she croaked.

I shifted my gaze to the table.

The pile of tiny paper scraps had vanished.

The poster had grown back—in one whole piece.

With the big white mantis-shaped spot in the middle.

18

I raised my eyes to the green ball.

It fell to the floor with a dull thump.

Two black feelers thrust out of the top.

Six long bristly legs burst out of the back.

The pincers on the front legs snapped open and closed.

"Get out!" I yelled at Lauren. "Get out while you can! The mantis is back!"

"I'm staying!" she shouted. "Where is it? What should I do?"

"It's coming this way. Circle around the table

and stand on the other side of the room. Maybe it won't be able to decide which of us to go for!"

Lauren slid around the table. "What's it doing now? Do you think it's going to attack?"

I backed up until I hit the wall. "It's so close I can't move." I gulped. "It's in a praying position."

"Wes, play dead!" Lauren cried. "It wants to eat food that's still alive!"

I slumped onto the floor and rolled my eyes back in my head. I tried to hold my breath.

For a second nothing happened. Then I felt the mantis's cold feelers probing my neck.

It's trying to decide if I'm alive, I thought. If I move a muscle, it will attack.

I could feel its hot breath on my cheek.

Its saliva drip down my face.

My eyelids twitched as its creepy pincers crawled along my skin.

I wanted to bat it away.

Don't move. Don't move.

I wanted to breathe. My chest felt tight. My lungs were about to burst.

Don't move! Don't move!

Slowly I felt the mantis slide away. I heard him slither in his drool across the kitchen floor.

I opened one eye.

I couldn't spot the mantis. Where was it?

My lungs were definitely going to explode now. I took a tiny breath. Then I opened my other eye and lifted my head slightly off the floor.

Now I could see it.

But Lauren couldn't. She was watching me. Biting her lip. Twisting her hands together. Worrying about me.

And there was the mantis—standing next to her. Standing next to Lauren—who was breathing. Moving. Alive.

I slowly pushed myself off the floor.

"Don't move!" I mouthed.

Lauren understood.

I crept over to the mantis. Slowly. Very slowly.

It was perched next to the stove. Rocking back and forth.

Rubbing its pincers together.

"Hey, what are you guys doing? Why are you crawling on the floor?" a voice called from the doorway.

Vicky.

The mantis snapped its head toward my sister. I grabbed Lauren's arm and pulled her away from the huge insect.

"Wow! Your glasses are ruined," Vicky said,

lifting the broken frames from the table. "Wes, you're in major trouble!"

The mantis's feelers waved with fury. Its eyes darted from me to Lauren to Vicky and back.

"I've never broken my glasses," Vicky bragged. "Never even lost them. Wait until Mom and Dad see." She pushed her glasses up.

I slid along the wall toward her. Then I jumped up, grabbed her glasses off her face, and pushed her away.

"Hey, what are you doing?" she yelled. "Those are mine!"

She tried to snatch them back.

"Ssh!" I warned. I held them high over my head.

She hopped up and down, but she couldn't reach them.

"Vicky, wait outside. I'll give them back in a minute," I promised.

"I'm not leaving without my glasses!" Vicky folded her arms in front of her. "And you'd better not break them!"

I forced her glasses on my face. They were way too small. They pinched my nose. And they didn't quite reach my ears.

"You look stupid," Vicky said.

"Quiet!" I warned. I had to concentrate.

I stared at the mantis.

I moved closer to it and stared really hard.

I strained to see every detail.

Focus. Focus. Don't blink.

I moved in closer.

I stared.

Disappear. Please—disappear back into the poster.

This *has* to work, I told myself. It *has* to.

But the mantis didn't move.

19

"The glasses aren't working!" I moaned. "They're just not working."

The mantis lashed out—so fast I didn't see it coming. But I felt it.

It had me by the neck. Choking off my air.

Its pincers raked my skin.

Its huge eyes gleamed greedily into mine.

Its jaws snapped open and shut. Then it lifted me right off the floor.

Lauren and Vicky gasped as I rose up.

"He's floating!" Vicky cried.

I kicked helplessly.

"Wes, you're scaring me!" Vicky cried.

"Keep staring, Wes! Keep staring!" Lauren yelled.

I gazed directly into the mantis's face. Colors swirled through its deep black eyes. Its eyes looked like two giant kaleidoscopes now. Swirling colors in orange, pink, yellow, green.

Swirling colors!

Colored dots!

"It's working!" I cried. "I think it's working!"

Vicky's glasses *were* working. They were weaker than mine—so they were just taking longer!

Fluorescent dots began to race over the mantis's legs and feelers. Over its whole body!

Then the dots drifted apart.

I crumpled to the floor, but I kept Vicky's glasses pressed against my face.

Dots bounced off the refrigerator. They hit the screen door. They whirled and swirled like mini-tornadoes through the kitchen.

"Give me my glasses back now," Vicky whined. "You're acting crazy."

"Just one more minute, Vicky," I begged. "One more minute." I knew I had almost defeated it.

"Wes! The poster!" Lauren exclaimed, dashing over to the table.

111

I forced myself up and peered over her shoulder.

The white mantis-shaped spot had filled in with color. The mantis was back where he belonged.

Sal had definitely been right. Some things *are* better left in two dimensions.

I collapsed into a kitchen chair.

"We won! We won!" Lauren cheered.

"Not yet." I sighed. "We still have to get rid of the poster."

"Give me my glasses back, Wes." Vicky stomped her feet on the floor.

"Not yet, Vicky," I murmured.

"I'll get Mom and Dad. They'll make you."

"Where are Mom and Dad?" I asked.

"They're outside in the front yard burning a pile of leaves," Vicky replied. Then she ran out, slamming the screen door behind her.

I turned to Lauren and smiled. I eyed the poster. "Let's burn it!"

"Yesss!" Lauren held up her palm and we high-fived.

We dashed out to the front yard. "Hi, Mom!" I called. "Where's Dad?"

"He's in the back, collecting more leaves," she answered. "Wes, what are you doing with your sister's glasses?" Vicky stood beside her—squinting at me triumphantly.

"Uhhh. It's part of a science project," I blurted out.

"For Mr. Gosling's class. Optics," Lauren added.

"Please let me wear them for five more minutes, Vicky," I pleaded.

"Let your brother wear them for a few minutes, Vicky. It's for school."

Vicky dug her foot into the dirt and kicked a chunk of it on my jeans.

"Come on, Vicky," Mom said, wrapping an arm around her shoulder. "Let's help Dad with the leaves in the backyard. Then we'll all go in and have some ice cream."

"Can I throw them into the fire? Can I have chocolate-banana-chunk? Can I give Clawd some?"

"No, yes, and yes," Mom replied as they made their way around back.

I peered up at the sky. It was almost dark. A full orange moon glowed above.

I turned to Lauren. "Okay," I said. "Here goes nothing." I tossed the poster into the center of the fire.

The flames caught on the edge of the poster. Then there was a bang—like a firecracker shooting off.

Lauren and I jumped back.

"Guess we're kind of nervous." Lauren giggled nervously. "I don't see anything weird happening. Do you?"

"No," I answered. Then I sniffed the air. It suddenly smelled bad. Really bad. Like the mantis's sour breath.

The fire engulfed the poster now. Furious flames shot through it and licked the sky.

Smoke began to stream from the center of the leaf pile. Greenish-gray smoke. It rose fast—in a long, straight ribbon.

Then I heard the high-pitched buzzing. Louder. Louder. Louder. I wanted to cover my ears. But I had to hold Vicky's glasses on.

Lauren glanced at me. "You okay?" she asked.

I nodded.

The smoke drifted higher in the sky. Drifted past the full, bright, orange moon. Then it began to curl.

The smoke curled and curled—into the form of a perfect praying mantis. Huge and dark, it floated in front of the moon.

Then it disappeared.

I turned to Lauren. "Did you see that?" I asked.

"See what?" she said.

"Never mind," I replied.

No one else could see the mantis.

No one else could hear its terrible buzzing.

No one else could make it come alive.

The mantis was my own private nightmare.

A nightmare in 3-D.

And it was over.

Or was it?

20

Two weeks later Lauren came home from school with me. We planned to do some homework together.

"Wes, you got a package today," Mom said when she walked into the kitchen. She set down a cylinder-shaped package on the kitchen table.

Lauren and I exchanged glances.

"The Mystery Prize!" we cried together.

We both dropped our pencils.

I picked the package up. I checked out the return address. "It's from the poster company," I told Lauren. "It's definitely my prize."

"Open it!" Lauren said.

I tore the wrapping off one end and slid the prize out of the cylinder.

"I can't believe it! Another poster!" I said. I rolled it open on the table.

"Oh, no!" Lauren gasped. "Careful, Wes," she said under her breath.

"Another stereogram?" Mom asked, looking over our shoulders. "Is that the prize? Can you see it, Lauren?"

Lauren squinted at the poster. "Uh-uh. I can't see a thing," she said. "Just those black and brown lines."

Mom spent a long time staring at it. But she couldn't make it out, either.

"Hey, what's up? Cool! Whose poster? What is it? Can I have a look?" It was Vicky, of course.

"Sure, have a look," I said, shoving the poster toward her.

"Nope. Can't see a thing. Mom, what's for dinner? Can I have a snack now? Please? Where's Clawd?"

"Pizza. No. In the backyard," Mom told Vicky.

Lauren moved closer. "Are you going to try to see it?" she whispered.

"Do you think I should?" I asked.

117

Lauren shrugged. "Might as well. We know how to control it, don't we?"

I leaned on the table and looked over the top of my glasses.

It took me only a few seconds to see it.

It was big.

And hairy.

And coming straight at me.

A gigantic tarantula scurried out from under a rock and reached a hairy leg right out of the poster.

I jumped backward and nearly fell over Vicky.

"Wes!" Mom cried. "What on earth is wrong with you?"

"Nothing, Mom. It's okay," I replied. I rolled the poster up as fast as I could. "Lauren, can you give me a hand with these books?" I asked.

When we got upstairs, I told her. "There's a monster in the poster. A huge tarantula. And, Lauren," I whispered, "it wants to get out!"

"Come on, Fluffy!" came a voice from next door.

Lauren and I peered out the window.

I saw Gabby. She and Corny were playing with Fluffums. This was the game: They had a stuffed cat, white like Clawd. It had a collar around its

118

neck and a leash. They were dragging the stuffed cat in a circle. They were urging Fluffums to chase it and catch it.

"Come on, Fluff," Corny instructed. "Get that nasty old cat."

Fluffums went running after the cat. He grabbed it and chewed on its neck, growling.

"Good boy!" Gabby cried, patting the dog.

It made me feel sick.

"I'm really starting to dislike that family," Lauren said.

The twins stared up at us. "Hey, where is your cross-eyed cat?" Corny called.

"Yeah, Fluffums wants to play!" Gabby added.

They were both twirling their ponytails and smirking.

I turned to Lauren. "I bet I can make them promise to keep that little hairball away from Clawd from now on."

I leaned out the window. "Hey, you guys, I forgot to tell you!" I shouted. "I won the prize. I solved the Mystery Stereogram."

"Yeah, for sure!" Gabby said, rolling her eyes.

"No way," Corny added.

I sighed and ducked back in the window.

"Bet they'd just love to see my prize," I said. I

tapped the tarantula poster on my hand. "Maybe I'll even give it to them."

"Good idea," Lauren replied, grinning evilly. "I'll hold your glasses this time. You don't want to break another pair."

"Corny! Gabby!" I called out the window. "Wait right there. I have a really cool surprise for you!"

GHOSTS of FEAR STREET ®

THE
BUGMAN LIVES!

1

"Hey, Janet! Want to see me jump the curb?" Carl Beemer *whooshed* past me on his Rollerblades.

I didn't look up from my weeding. I didn't want to watch Carl jump the curb. I didn't want to watch him do anything—except skate away.

Carl is a pain. All he does is brag, brag, brag.

Carl zoomed up the front walk and stopped next to me. "Having fun?" he taunted.

Ignore him, I told myself. Maybe he'll leave. I kept working on the flower bed. Jabbing at the dirt and pulling out the weeds.

"I bet you aren't getting paid for that, are you?" Carl asked.

I wasn't. Mom says weeding is part of my family responsibilities. But Carl didn't have to know that. "None of your business," I muttered.

Carl laughed. "You aren't," he guessed.

I felt my face get hot. I hate it when Carl is right.

Carl stuck one of his big feet in front of me. "See my new Rollerblades? Cool, huh? I paid for them myself. I'm making big bucks with my mowing business."

I sat back in the grass and stared up at him. "Really? Maybe I'll get some jobs, too." If Carl could make money mowing lawns, I knew I could. I can do anything Carl can do—except better.

"Yeah, right," Carl answered. "Who would hire you?"

"Lots of people," I shot back. "By the end of the week I'll have more jobs than you do."

"No way!" Carl protested.

"Remember the recycling contest at school?" I asked. "I brought in eighteen more pounds of paper than you did."

Carl snorted. He sounds like a hog when he does that. "If I knew old telephone books counted, I would have beat you."

"Janet," Mom called from the house. "Are you getting those flower beds weeded?"

2

"Almost done!" I yelled back.

Carl snickered. "Yeah, Janet. Just think of all the money you're making doing that weeding." He skated off.

I rocked forward onto my knees again and started yanking up the weeds as fast as I could. I had to find some mowing jobs right away. I wanted *twice* as many as Carl had.

If I earned enough money, maybe I could go to camp next year like my friends. Then I wouldn't have to spend another summer in Shadyside with only Carl Beemer for company.

I scooped up all the weeds and stuffed them in a big plastic bag. "Mom!" I yelled. "I'm done. I'm going for a walk, okay?"

"See you later," she called.

I rushed over to our next-door neighbor's house. I combed my short, curly brown hair with my fingers and brushed the dirt off my shorts. Then I rang the bell.

Mrs. Kemp opened the door and peered at me through the screen.

"Hi, Mrs. Kemp," I said. "Do you need someone to mow your lawn this summer? I'm a good mower."

Mrs. Kemp smiled. "Sorry, Janet. I have a lawn service that does all my yard work."

"Oh," I said, feeling disappointed. "Well, thanks

3

anyway." I hurried back to the sidewalk. At least Carl didn't see that, I thought.

Then I heard him laughing. Carl popped out from behind the big oak tree in Mrs. Kemp's yard. "I'm a good mower," he squeaked in a high little voice.

"I don't sound like that!" I exclaimed.

"I don't sound like that!" Carl squeaked.

I stomped over to the next house. I heard the *shoop shoop* of Carl's skates behind me.

Why isn't Carl at camp this summer like Anita and Sara? I thought. Or at the Grand Canyon with his family like my best friend, Megan? Or visiting his grandmother like Toad?

Why does he have to be the one kid in the neighborhood—besides me—who is stuck spending the summer in Shadyside?

I rushed up to the Hoffmans' door. They didn't need their lawn mowed, either. And neither did the Hasslers, the Martins, or the Prescotts.

But I refused to give up. Especially with Carl watching.

I trooped through the neighborhood trying every house. Everyone told me they mowed their own lawn or they had already hired someone.

One guy had already hired *Carl.* Of course, Carl didn't bother to tell me that before I went to the door and asked. The jerk.

4

"You're striking out big time," Carl informed me. "You can't get a job anywhere!"

It took all my strength to keep from turning around and knocking his head off. "Why do you keep following me?" I demanded. "Go away. Get a life."

But he stayed right behind me. Of course. Carl never did anything I wanted him to.

I turned the corner—and heard Carl give a big gasp.

"*Ooooo*—Fear Street!" he teased. I glanced back at him. He had both his hands stuffed in his mouth, pretending to bite off all his fingernails.

Carl thinks he is hilarious. I shook my head as I started toward the first house.

This place definitely needs my help, I thought. High grass covered most of the crooked stone walkway. Weeds were taking over the flower beds. And dark green ivy clung to the porch railing and the front of the house.

I climbed the porch steps and rang the bell. A woman about my mom's age opened the door. She had short black hair, and she looked friendly.

"Hi," I said. "My name is Janet Monroe. I wondered if you need someone to mow your lawn this summer."

She smiled. I noticed she had a little gap between

5

her top two teeth. "That would be wonderful. I've been looking in the paper for someone to help me with the yard. Your timing is perfect."

"Fantastic!" I exclaimed.

"I'm Iris Lowy," the woman said. "When can you start, Janet? As you can see, my yard needs a *lot* of work." We both laughed.

"I can start right now," I told her.

"Great. How much do you charge?"

"Umm, four-fifty an hour," I said. I hoped that was okay. I hadn't thought about how much to ask for.

"Sounds fair," Mrs. Lowy answered. "The lawn mower is in the garage." She pointed around to the side of the house.

"Thanks," I said. As soon as she closed the door, I turned and grinned at Carl.

"So you got one lousy job," Carl taunted. "Big deal." He skated off down the street.

Finally, I thought. At least he isn't hanging around to watch me work.

I trotted up to the garage and wheeled out the mower. An old gas one. The kind you have to start by pulling a cord.

I hauled it through a wooden gate and into the side yard. I sighed as I gazed at the long strip of overgrown grass.

6

You wanted a job, I reminded myself. I yanked on the pull cord. Nothing.

I gave the cord another yank. Nothing.

"Come on, come on," I muttered.

I jerked the cord again. The motor blasted into action. The vibration raced up my hands and through my body.

I leaned my weight into the mower and pushed. I could feel the muscles in the backs of my legs strain as I struggled across the side yard.

The air was so heavy and hot I could hardly breathe. Sweat slid down my back. It trickled down my forehead and dripped into my eyes.

I knew Carl would love it if I quit, so I pictured him watching me with a stupid grin on his face. That helped me keep mowing.

My palms burned and itched against the handle of the mower. By the time I finished the side yard, I could feel blisters forming on both of them. And my hands are pretty tough.

I stopped the mower, letting the engine idle. I wiped my face on my sleeve and took in a deep breath. I love the smell of freshly cut grass.

I shook my arms out at my sides. My muscles already felt sore—and I had barely started.

I rolled the mower around to the backyard.

That's when I saw it.

A huge, tangled mass of tall weeds and grass in the far corner of the yard.

The rectangle-shaped patch wasn't that big—it looked about the size of the rug we have in our front hallway. But some of the weeds grew higher than my waist.

I should get it over with, I decided. I dragged the mower over to the patch.

Hundreds of tiny black bugs buzzed in the grass. And some of the weeds looked really prickly.

You can do it, I told myself. I aimed the mower at the patch and shoved as hard as I could.

The grass tangled around my knees. Thistles scratched my legs. I could feel the little bugs crawling over my bare skin.

Wheer! The mower squealed as I forced it through the patch. My muscles trembled with the effort.

The scream of the mower grew louder and louder. I didn't think I could stand another second of it. I wanted to cover my ears.

I slammed myself against the mower. Giving it one last huge shove.

Crack!

The mower bashed into something.

The motor groaned to a stop.

What happened? What made that horrible cracking sound?

I pulled the mower back and crouched down. I

8

shoved the grass back with my hands and found a stone.

A large, flat stone.

I ran my fingers over it. It felt icy cold. And smooth.

Then I felt deep grooves. I pushed more grass out of the way. And I saw the word HERE chiseled into the stone.

I yanked away clumps of weeds with both hands until I uncovered the whole stone.

It was one of the hottest days of the summer—but a cold shiver ran up my back when I read the words carved there.

HERE LIES THE BUGMAN. WOE TO ANYONE WHO WAKES HIM.

2

I jumped up.

A tombstone? I thought. Someone is *buried* under there. I'm standing on a grave.

I backed away. My feet got tangled in the weeds and I hit the ground hard.

I could feel weeds poking into my back. A swarm of tiny black gnats hovered above my face.

I'm on a grave, I thought.

I fell right on top of a grave. My heart thudded. I scrambled to my feet. And looked down.

HERE LIES THE BUGMAN. WOE TO ANYONE WHO WAKES HIM.

Right through the stone was a big jagged crack. A crack I made.

I turned and ran to Mrs. Lowy's back door. I pounded on it.

Mrs. Lowy jerked the door open. "Janet, what happened?" she asked. "Are you hurt?"

"I think I ran over a tombstone with the mower and broke it," I said. All my words ran together.

"What?" Mrs. Lowy cried. "A tombstone?"

I pulled in a deep breath and tried to talk more slowly. "I was mowing that overgrown patch in the side over there and I hit something. I think it's a tombstone."

"It can't be," Mrs. Lowy said. "Show me."

"Okay." I led the way back over to the stone and pointed down at it. My hand was shaking.

"My, my," Mrs. Lowy said. "I would have been scared if I found that, too. But it has to be a joke. Some teenagers probably heard those old stories about the Bugman and thought it would be funny."

"What stories?" I asked.

"Oh, you know. Stories about the man who used to live in the house next door years and years ago," she told me.

I shook my head. I still didn't know what she was talking about.

"Everyone called him the Bugman. He was fascinated by bugs and spent all his time studying them,"

Mrs. Lowy continued. "He was odd—didn't go out much or talk to his neighbors. People said he eventually turned into a bug himself."

"That's creepy." I wrapped my arms tightly around myself.

"Well, you know how everyone likes to tell stories about Fear Street," Mrs. Lowy said. "I'm sure someone put that stone there as a prank. I've never seen it before. And I've lived here for five years."

I nodded and tried to smile. I didn't want Mrs. Lowy to think I was a baby.

"Don't bother to finish that spot," Mrs. Lowy said. "It's not part of my yard anyway. It belongs to the house next door. Whoever ends up buying the house can deal with it."

"You mean no one lives there?" I glanced over at the other house. It was in worse shape than Mrs. Lowy's.

"It's been empty for years. I wish someone would take it. It would be nice to have neighbors." Mrs. Lowy sighed. "Do you want a Coke or anything before you go back to work?" she asked.

"No, thanks," I told her. I wanted to get out of there—fast.

"If you change your mind, let me know," Mrs. Lowy called as she headed back to the house.

I grabbed the mower handle. I ignored the blisters

on my hands, my sore arms and legs, and the heat. All I cared about was finishing the job so I could leave. I turned the mower around and went back to work.

But I couldn't stop thinking about the tombstone. The word *Bugman* pounded in my head with every step.

Bugman.

Bugman.

Bugman.

"Come on, Janet," I said to myself. "Chill out." I decided to check the tombstone. Maybe it wasn't as bad as I thought.

I left the mower running and rushed over to the stone. The huge crack was still there. The stone was split in half.

I read the words again. HERE LIES THE BUGMAN. WOE TO ANYONE WHO WAKES HIM.

What if I did wake him? What if he climbed out of his grave? What if he's watching me right now? What if—

Stop it, I ordered myself. I marched back over to the mower. Mrs. Lowy is right. The tombstone is just a stupid joke.

I glanced at it over my shoulder. Nothing.

I pushed the mower a little farther. Then I looked back at the tombstone again. Nothing.

It's going to take all day if I keep stopping to make sure the Bugman isn't coming out of his tomb! I thought.

"So you finally finished," Carl called. "Took you long enough." He jumped out of the cedar tree in my front yard and landed right in front of me.

I groaned. "Carl, don't you have a home?"

"Mowing is hard work. I bet you're ready to quit. If they want you to do the lawn again, you can give them my number," Carl volunteered.

"No way!" I plopped down on the grass and picked off some of the thistles stuck to my shorts. "Mrs. Lowy already hired me for the rest of the summer. She wants me to weed and water, too."

Carl sat down with his back against the tree trunk. "How did you get all those little cuts?"

Talking to Carl is better than talking to nobody, I decided. A little better.

"One spot in the backyard had all this high grass and weeds and thistles," I answered. "Something weird happened when I started mowing it. I ran into a big stone—"

"That was stupid," Carl said. "You could have busted the mower."

I ignored him. "It looked like a tombstone. It had words carved on it—'Here Lies the Bugman. Woe to

Anyone Who Wakes Him.' And I cracked it right down the middle."

"So?" Carl said, trying to sound bored.

"Mrs. Lowy—the lady who hired me—said this guy called the Bugman lived in the house next door to her more than fifty years ago," I explained. "He studied bugs—and some people thought he was turning into one."

"And you cracked open his tombstone?" Carl asked. "Aren't you scared? The tombstone said 'Woe to anyone who wakes him.' That means you."

Carl sounded happy. "Woe! Woe! Woe! Woe!" he chanted.

Why do I bother talking to him? "Mrs. Lowy thinks some kids put the tombstone there as a joke," I said.

"And you believed her?" Carl asked. "Adults always tell kids stuff like that. She probably didn't want you to get scared."

"I wasn't scared," I said quickly. "It's just an old story." No way was I admitting the truth to Carl.

"You should be scared," Carl warned. "I've heard of the Bugman. My uncle Rich told me about him. He could control insects. He could make them do anything he wanted. Sting people. Or spy on them and report back. Or—"

"Oh, right," I snapped. I studied Carl's face. He could be making the whole thing up to torture me.

Or he could be telling the truth.

"Really," Carl insisted. "I heard about some kids who cut across his lawn once—and a whole swarm of wasps went after them. They got about a million stings each. And cracking his tombstone is a lot worse than walking on his lawn."

"Even if that story is true—and it isn't—the Bugman is dead now," I told him. "He's been dead for a long time."

"Yeah, you're right," Carl said. "I guess he can't do anything to you."

"I'm going in to get something to drink," I announced. I stood up. Expecting Carl to tag along—as usual.

But he didn't move. He stared up at me. His mouth hanging open. His gray eyes bulging. Not a pretty sight.

"What?" I asked.

"Freeze," he whispered. "It's starting."

Carl sounded scared. I felt my stomach twist. *"What?"*

Carl slowly pushed himself to his feet. "There is a giant wasp crawling on your shoulder. It has to be one of *his*. The Bugman is after you."

3

"**D**on't move," Carl said in a low voice, creeping closer.

"Just get it off," I whispered. I didn't know how much longer I could stand still.

"It's crawling around your back now," he whispered. "Hold it, hold it. Don't move. There!"

Whap! Carl smacked his hand down on my back—hard!

"Ha, ha! You really fell for that one!" Carl cried. He cracked up. "Get it off! Get it off!" he squeaked in that high little voice that is supposed to sound like mine.

I hate Carl. I really, really hate him.

"You jerk!" I shouted. I gave him a hard punch on the shoulder. Then I stalked into the house and slammed the door behind me.

Carl made up that whole stupid story, I reminded myself when I rode up to Mrs. Lowy's house two days later. And that tombstone is a fake. Just a dumb joke.

I parked my bike in the side yard and hurried into the garage to get gardening tools. Mrs. Lowy wasn't home—but I found the tools right where she said I would. Good.

I'll start with that bed of red and white flowers near the big tree in the front yard, I decided. I ambled over and sat down in the shade. Then I pulled on a pair of gardening gloves—I wanted to protect my hands. I had tons of blisters from all the mowing.

Weeding for money is a lot more fun than weeding for free, I thought as I worked. And in the front yard I didn't have to look at the tombstone.

My eyes wandered over to the old reddish-brown house next door. The paint was flaking off in spots, exposing a coat of dingy white paint underneath. It reminded me of somebody's skin peeling after a bad sunburn.

I turned back to the weeding. How did all the stories about the Bugman get started? I wondered.

I yanked up weed after weed. Maybe the Bugman was a scientist, I thought. That's why he spent all his time with bugs.

Or maybe his name was something like Buckman—and some little kid misunderstood it. That could have started all the weird stories. I gathered up a bunch of the weeds and stuffed them in a garbage bag.

My body felt sore all over. I pulled off my gloves and stood up. I stretched my arms over my head as high as I could, going all the way up on my toes.

Wait. I spotted someone in one of the upper-story windows next door. Someone staring down at me.

I dropped back down on my heels. Is someone in that house? It's supposed to be empty.

A drop of sweat rolled into one of my eyes. I wiped my face with the hem of my T-shirt and stared back at the house.

The curtain in the window fluttered.

I kept watching. Waiting.

No movement. Nothing.

I must have imagined it.

Back to work, I thought. I wiped my face again. Then plopped back down on the grass and pulled on one of the gardening gloves.

19

"Oww!" I shouted. Something jabbed into my finger. I yanked off the glove.

A bee! I got stung by a bee! It must have crawled inside the glove.

My finger was already red and swollen.

I jumped to my feet, shaking my hand back and forth. Trying to cool off my stinging finger.

I should run it under the hose, I thought. I dashed toward the garage—and tripped on the stone walkway.

"Are you hurt?" someone asked.

I looked up. A man loomed over me. He leaned down and peered at me through his thick, thick glasses. His eyes were huge. The biggest eyes I ever saw.

The hair on my arms stood up. The man's unblinking black eyes gave me the creeps.

"Are you all right?" he asked in a thin, high voice. "I heard you yell, then I saw you fall."

"I got a bee sting on my finger," I explained. "I was running over to the hose and I tripped."

He held out his hand. It was long and thin, and covered by a brown work glove.

I pretended I didn't notice it and stood up. The pain in my sore finger was killing me.

"Come on. I'll get you some ice," he said.

Ice would feel great on the sting. "Thanks," I answered.

He led the way across the lawn. I slowed down when I realized where he was headed. The old deserted house next door. I *did* see someone over there, I thought.

The man glanced at me curiously, so I sped up again. I shot a quick look at him. He must be hot in all those clothes. He wore a baggy long-sleeved black shirt buttoned all the way to the top, long green pants, and a floppy brown hat.

Not one speck of skin showed. Except for his face.

Weird, I thought. I stopped in the front of the porch. "Um, Mrs. Lowy told me no one lived here," I said.

"I just moved in yesterday," he answered. "I'm Mr. Cooney and I'm renting the house for the summer. I'll be right back with the ice. Sit down." He gestured to a couple of wicker chairs on the porch.

"Thanks." I could hear him humming to himself as he disappeared through the screen door. I peered after him, but I couldn't see inside the house.

A few minutes later Mr. Cooney came back out the screen door. He carried a tray with a pitcher, two glasses, and a little plastic bag full of ice.

He set the tray down and handed me the ice. "That should take the sting out," he said.

I pressed the ice against my finger. The skin started getting numb right away.

"Would you like some juice?" he asked. He held up a pitcher filled with green liquid.

"What kind is it?" I asked.

"Oh, it's a mixture of fresh fruits. I'm a health-food nut."

"Okay, great," I said.

He picked up a glass and filled it almost to the top. He handed it to me, then poured a glass for himself.

"Oh, my name's Janet Monroe," I told him. I set the juice on the porch rail so I could hold the ice on my finger.

"Do you live next door?" he asked, then took a long gulp of his juice.

"No. I don't live on Fear Street. The lady who lives here hired me to do yard work," I explained.

He gazed at me through his thick glasses. "This house is quite run down, as you can see," Mr. Cooney said. "The yard needs a lot of attention. Would you be interested in doing some work for me, too?"

"That would be great!" I exclaimed. I couldn't wait to tell Carl. He's going to be sorry he gave me the idea of doing yard work, I thought. Between this place and Mrs. Lowy's, I'll be making a ton of money.

Mr. Cooney smiled. "Drink your juice," he urged.

"It looks strange, but it tastes good. You can get dehydrated working in the sun all day."

I was thirsty. I set down the ice and picked up the glass. I tilted my head back, closed my eyes, and gulped down the juice.

The cold, sweet liquid felt so good.

I opened my eyes. Something brushed against my top lip, something was going into my mouth. Something prickly. I crossed my eyes, trying to see what it was.

Something dark. Something shiny.

Something alive.

4

Gross!

My stomach lurched. I spit the rest of the juice over the porch railing.

"A *beetle!*" I shrieked. "There's a beetle in my juice! And it's alive!"

Coughing and choking, I stared into the glass at the huge bug. Its wings dripped with the sticky green juice.

I dropped the glass and scrubbed my mouth with my fingers. Hard. I couldn't get the feel of that disgusting beetle off my lips.

I squeezed past Mr. Cooney. I spotted a hose near

the side of the house and raced over to it. Then I turned it on full blast.

I took a huge gulp of water. I swished it around in my mouth and spit. If I didn't get rid of that horrible feeling, I would be sick right there.

"Sorry," Mr. Cooney called from the porch. "It must have fallen in the pitcher."

I went back to the porch, picked up the glass, and reached out to drop the beetle on the ground.

"Don't!" Mr. Cooney screeched. His eyes glistened behind his glasses.

I stopped, startled.

"I'll take care of it," he continued more softly.

I handed him the glass. He carefully fished the beetle out and put it on the porch railing.

Mr. Cooney set the glass on the porch railing, too. "So, Janet, when can you start work?" he asked.

"Is tomorrow okay?" I wanted to go to the town pool after I finished Mrs. Lowy's weeding.

"Sure," he answered. "See you then."

I rode my bike straight from Mrs. Lowy's to the pool. I spread some sunscreen on my arms and legs. Then I stretched out on my big black and white beach towel. The one I got free for being the first caller to answer KLIV's music trivia question.

Some little kids splashed around in the wading pool. A few seventh graders I recognized took turns on the high dive. And a couple of guys stood around talking to the teenage girl on lifeguard duty. But I couldn't find one person I knew to hang out with.

I wish Megan would hurry up and get back from vacation, I thought. It's not that fun spending the afternoon at the pool with no one to talk to.

Oh, well. It's a lot better than weeding and mowing, I reminded myself. I closed my eyes. Enjoying the hot sun on my skin.

I like to wait until I can't stand being in the sun one more second. Then I jump right into the deep end. The cold water feels great.

Whap!

"Ow!" My stomach stung like crazy.

I didn't even have to open my eyes to know what happened. "You're dead, Carl!" I yelled. I sat up and grabbed his towel away before he could snap me with it again.

Carl laughed. "I'm sooo scared," he answered. Then he cannonballed into the pool.

Whoosh! The giant wave Carl created drenched me. "Jerk," I muttered.

Carl came up for air. Still laughing.

I leaned over and splashed water into his face until he started to choke. The lifeguard gave me a dirty look—so I stopped.

Carl hoisted himself out of the pool and plopped down next to me.

26

"I got another mowing job," I announced before he could say a word.

"Two jobs. Big deal." Carl snorted.

"Yeah, but my new job is huge. I'll be working tons—a lot more than you," I told him.

"Where is this *huge* job?" Carl demanded.

I hesitated. "Next door to Mrs. Lowy," I said.

"The *Bugman's* house?" Carl yelled. "You're working for the Bugman?"

"I'm not working for the Bugman," I protested. "I'm working for Mr. Cooney. He lives in the house where the Bugman *used* to live. The Bugman is dead—get it?"

"Big mistake," Carl said. He pointed to my leg. "Look! He sent another one of his bug friends after you."

My heart give a hard *thump*.

I felt tiny legs traveling toward my knee.

I didn't want to look. But I forced myself to glance down.

A ladybug. That's all. A little red and black ladybug crawling up my leg.

I reached down to flick it off.

"Noooooo!" someone screamed.

5

~~~

"**D**on't do that! You'll be sorry." A girl in a purple and yellow bathing suit ran toward me. "Noooo!" she screamed. "Don't do it. Leave that ladybug alone. It's bad luck."

The girl threw herself down next to me. She stuck her finger in front of the ladybug—and it crawled right on. "Poor baby," she crooned.

Carl snorted.

I didn't even glance at him. This strange girl was talking to a bug.

She looked up at me. "Sorry if I scared you by

yelling like that," the girl apologized. "But I couldn't let you hurt this little ladybug."

"It's a bug," Carl said loudly. "A stupid bug. What's your problem?"

"Every creature on earth deserves life," she told us. "That's what my whole family believes. We don't eat meat or fish or eggs. Even our cat is a vegetarian."

"Sorry," I mumbled. "I wasn't really trying to kill it. I just wanted it off me."

The girl nodded. "Most people don't ever think about bugs," she said. "If they did, they would probably treat them better."

The ladybug flew off the girl's finger. She gave it a little wave.

"What about spiders?" Carl demanded. "Or centipedes? I bet you kill them."

"I don't believe in murder," the girl answered. "When you kill anything—even a spider—you upset the balance of the universe."

Carl snorted again.

"Did you know you sound like a pig when you do that?" the girl asked.

I laughed. That's exactly what I think every time Carl gives one of his snorts.

She's cool, I decided. Weird—but cool, too. And she has to be more fun than Carl.

"I'm Janet," I told the girl. "And he's Carl."

"I'm Willow," the girl said.

"What grade are you in?" I asked. "I've never seen you at school."

"I'm going into sixth," Willow answered. "But I do home study. My family believes you can learn everything you need to know from the world around you."

Carl slid up to the edge of the pool and dangled his feet in the water. Ignoring us.

"So your parents teach you? Isn't that—" I began.

"Look!" Carl exclaimed. "There's an ant in the water. It's going to drown."

Willow scrambled next to Carl. "Where?"

"Right there!" he cried. "A big black one."

Willow leaned forward—and Carl started kicking as hard as he could. Splashing water into Willow's face.

"Carl, you idiot!" I yelled.

Willow jumped into the pool. She grabbed Carl by both feet and yanked him into the water.

Carl came up sputtering. He lunged for Willow.

She twisted to the side—then dunked him again.

Definitely a cool girl, I thought.

"Say you're sorry!" Willow demanded.

"No way!" Carl choked out.

Dunk!

"Say it!" Willow ordered.

Carl shook his head. The stubborn expression on his face cracked me up.

Dunk!

"Okay, okay!" Carl shouted. "I'm *soooo* sorry. Are you happy now?"

"Yes," Willow told him calmly. She climbed out of the pool and sat down next to me.

"Why don't you take your new friend to the Bugman's house?" Carl urged me. "I bet they would get along great."

"Why don't you go see how long you can hold your breath under water?" I called back.

But Carl swung out of the pool and plopped himself down. He can't take a hint.

"Who's the Bugman?" Willow asked.

"He's a guy who loved bugs so much he turned into one," Carl told her. "So you better watch out. You could start growing extra legs any day." He gave Willow his best evil grin.

"Ignore him. It's just a dumb story," I protested.

The lifeguard blew her whistle. "Three o'clock," she announced. "Time for lap swimmers only. Everyone else out of the pool."

"I didn't know it was so late," Willow said. "I've got to go." She jumped up. "See you around," she called to me as she headed toward the locker room. "I come to the pool a lot."

31

Maybe this summer won't be so bad, I thought. I've got two jobs. And maybe I've found someone I can hang out with. Someone who *isn't* Carl.

I showed up at Mr. Cooney's early the next morning. I wanted to be done in time to go to the pool. I hoped Willow would be there again.

Mr. Cooney waved to me from the front porch. "I got the lawn mower out for you," he called. He pointed to a rusty mower by the porch steps.

I strolled over to it. No motor. Great, I thought. Just great.

"Do you want to borrow a long-sleeved shirt?" Mr. Cooney asked, peering down at me through those extra-thick glasses. "It isn't good for you to get too much sun, you know."

No way would Mr. Cooney ever get sunburned. He had on the same outfit as yesterday. Long pants, long-sleeved shirt buttoned all the way up, work gloves, and a hat.

Very strange guy. "No, thanks," I answered. I grabbed the mower handle. "My mom always makes me put on sunscreen."

"Okay." Mr. Cooney wandered back into the house. Humming to himself. Not a song. Just the same note over and over. *Hmm. Hmm. Hmm.*

I shook my head. He should get a Walkman, I thought.

I attacked the lawn. Pushing myself to mow as fast as I could.

By the time I finished, my T-shirt was glued to my back. I knew my face had to be bright red.

I checked my watch. Almost 2:10. If I hurried I could make it to the pool before 2:30.

But first I had to get paid.

I stared up at the big, old house. The curtains were drawn in every window. He must really hate the sun, I thought. I would hate to live in the dark that way.

I climbed up the porch steps. The heavy front door stood open beyond the screen. I knocked on the doorframe.

Quiet. No footsteps heading toward the door. Nothing.

I knocked again—harder.

He's got to be home, I thought. I know it. I would have noticed him leave.

I pressed my face against the screen door. But I still couldn't see anything. Too dark inside.

"Mr. Cooney?" I called. "I need to leave now!"

No answer.

I opened the door and stepped inside. The house smelled damp. Moldy.

My eyes adjusted to the dim room. A thick layer of dust covered everything—the warped wood floor, the flowered sofa, the green curtains. And there were no lamps anywhere.

This place is really creepy, I thought.

"Mr. Cooney?" I called again.

I walked down the hall.

Nothing. A door ahead of me was open a crack. I headed for it. All I wanted to do was get my money and get out of there.

I knocked on the door and it swung all the way open. I stepped inside.

There was Mr. Cooney, by a long table at the other end of the room. His back to me.

"How are you feeling today, hmm? You look well," he crooned in his high voice.

I stared around the dimly lit room. I didn't see anyone but Mr. Cooney.

"Yesss. Yesss. You are looking much better, my baby," he murmured. He turned slightly.

He raised his hand up in front of him.

Something sat there. Something black. Something hairy.

A tarantula!

Mr. Cooney brought the huge spider close to his lips.

Closer. Closer.

Then he did something that made me feel sick.

6

~~~

He kissed the spider!

How could he stand kissing a tarantula? How could he stand feeling that bristly black hair against his lips?

"I love you, my baby," Mr. Cooney cooed in his high voice. He kissed the giant spider again.

I gasped. I couldn't help it.

Mr. Cooney jerked his head toward me.

He strode across the room. The tarantula still in his hand.

I took a step backward—and bumped into the

doorjamb. "K-keep it away from me," I stammered. "Please."

Mr. Cooney stopped. "Oh!" he exclaimed. He returned to the table and set the tarantula down.

"I forget that everyone isn't as comfortable around spiders as I am," he apologized when he turned to face me again.

"Um, it's okay," I said in a rush. "I finished mowing the lawns. And . . . uh . . . I came to get paid."

I could hardly look at him. I'll just pretend I didn't see anything, I decided. What else could I do? Tell him what a cute spider he had? Yeah, right.

"That's fine," he answered. He didn't sound embarrassed or anything. He pulled out his wallet and handed me my pay. I put it in my pack. "Have a glass of juice before you go."

I nervously scanned the floor. Why does he have a tarantula? Does he have more than one of those spiders? I wanted out of there. Now.

"No, thanks," I blurted. "I—I have some water with me, and—"

"But your water must be warm by now," Mr. Cooney interrupted. He picked a pitcher up off the table and poured me a tall glass of the green juice.

He held the glass out to me. "Take it. It's a particularly good batch today."

I took the glass, checked it for bugs, then drank the juice in three big gulps.

I handed him the empty glass. "Thanks. I have to go. See you." I turned and rushed through the living room.

"I'll see you tomorrow," Mr. Cooney called as I slammed the screen door. Not if I see you first, I thought.

I jumped off the porch. I climbed on my bike and pedaled down the street as hard as I could.

Does he let that tarantula wander around his whole house? I wondered. I decided never to go inside again—just in case. Mr. Cooney could pay me out on the porch from now on.

He told that tarantula he loved it, I thought. That's so gross.

Suddenly I remembered what Mrs. Lowy told me about the Bugman. The Bugman loved bugs so much he started turning into one.

He *loved* bugs. And so did Mr. Cooney.

"Janet!" someone yelled.

I slowed down and glanced over my shoulder. Willow stood on the sidewalk.

I put on my brakes and jumped off the bike. "Didn't you hear me the first three times?" Willow complained.

"Sorry," I mumbled.

37

"Hey, what's wrong?" Willow asked. "You're all pale."

"It's sort of a long story," I told her. "Can you come over? I only live a couple blocks away."

"Sure," Willow answered. "I was heading over to the pool. But I can go later."

We started down the block. I walked my bike so we could talk. "You said you never heard of the Bugman, right?" I asked.

Willow nodded. Her green eyes serious.

"I hadn't, either. Until a couple days ago. . . ." I told her the whole story as we walked to my house.

Willow kicked a rock down the sidewalk. "You're giving me the creeps," she said when I got to the part about the Bugman turning into a bug. "You don't believe that story, do you?"

"No. And Mrs. Lowy said the tombstone had to be a joke. But here's the really weird part. Something really strange happened today."

We turned onto my front walk, and then I heard a familiar sound. *Shoop shoop. Shoop shoop.*

Great, I thought. All I need right now is Carl.

He zoomed past on his Rollerblades, then spun to a stop in front of us. "So what are we doing today?"

"What do you mean *we?*" I asked.

He acted as if he hadn't heard me. "You got any cookies?" He plopped down on the front porch and pulled off his skates.

"No. Go away." I rolled my eyes at Willow. She rolled her eyes back at me.

"Chips are okay then," Carl said. He stood up and walked into my house. Heading straight for the kitchen.

"Where did you find Junk Food Boy?" Willow whispered as we followed him.

"His mom and my mom are best friends," I explained. "I've known him since preschool. And I still haven't figured out how to get rid of him."

"Is that you, Janet?" my mother called from upstairs.

"Yeah!" I shouted back. "I brought a friend home. And Carl."

Willow giggled. "And Carl," she repeated.

"Make yourselves a snack," Mom answered.

Carl already had his head stuck in our refrigerator.

"So how is the Bugman?" Carl asked. He slammed the fridge door shut and opened one of the cupboards.

I didn't answer. Willow and I sat down at the kitchen table. "Come on," she urged. "Tell me what happened."

Carl grabbed a bag of Fritos and ripped it open with his teeth. He sat down across from us and shoved a handful of the corn chips in his mouth. "Something happened?" he mumbled.

39

"Yeah." I turned to Willow. "Today when it was time to leave, I went inside to find Mr. Cooney."

I felt the back of my neck prickle. I was getting the creeps just thinking about what happened.

"I heard him talking to someone, but no one else was in the room." I glanced back and forth between Willow and Carl. "You won't believe what he was talking to," I continued.

The prickly feeling moved up the back of my head.

"A tarantula!" Carl cried.

"How did you know?" I demanded.

My ear started to itch. I reached up to scratch it.

"Don't!" Carl hollered.

"I'm not falling for that stupid joke again," I snapped.

"It's not a joke," Willow said quietly.

Something soft touched my cheek.

Then I caught sight of something black. Something long, and black, and hairy. Walking across my face.

7

A tarantula. A tarantula was on my face, walking onto my eyebrow.

I squeezed my eyes shut.

"Hold still," Carl said. He picked up the newspaper from the kitchen table. "I'm going to knock it off you."

"No!" Willow exclaimed. "I'll get something to put it in."

She raced over and threw open the cabinet doors—one after the other. "Don't be afraid," she called. "It won't bite you unless you scare it. And

41

they aren't poisonous. Well, not poisonous enough to kill you."

The tarantula stepped onto my nose. Its bushy hair tickled my left nostril.

I heard Willow run back over to me. "You're okay," she said soothingly. "It's more afraid of you than you are of it."

I opened my eyes. Willow smiled in encouragement. She pressed a Tupperware container against my cheek. The she nudged the tarantula inside.

Whew!

"Put on the lid!" Carl ordered.

Willow held the lid against the container. "I can't seal it," she said. "The tarantula needs air."

I started to shake.

"It's all over," Willow said. "I'm going to make you a health shake. It will help you calm down," she added.

She picked up her purple and yellow backpack and hurried over to the kitchen counter.

I shoved my fingers through my hair. I scratched my scalp. I rubbed my face until my skin felt sore and hot. I brushed off my arms and legs.

But I kept feeling those spider legs crawling over me. Crawling everywhere. I stood up. "Carl, is there anything on my back?" I asked.

"No," he answered. His voice serious.

I studied the front of my shirt and arms and legs. Then I sat back down.

"Is it okay if I use your blender?" Willow asked.

"Yeah," I said. "There's fruit and stuff in the fridge."

"Whoa," Carl mumbled. He shook his head back and forth. "Whoa."

I stared down at the Tupperware container. I could see the tarantula moving around through the thick plastic.

Brraaap. Willow ran the blender at high speed.

A couple of minutes later she returned to the table with two thick, pale green shakes—and a Coke. She handed one of the shakes to me and the Coke to Carl. "Health shakes don't go with Fritos," she told him.

"Lucky for me," Carl answered.

"This is so weird," I muttered. "First I see a tarantula at Mr. Cooney's place. Then there's one here."

"It must have fallen into your backpack," Willow said.

"But that's not the weird part," I said. "Don't you think it's weird that a man who loves bugs would move into the Bugman's house?"

"There's only one thing that explains it," Carl said slowly.

"What?" I finally asked.

"Mr. Cooney *is* the Bugman," he answered.

"You moron," I snapped. "The Bugman is dead! That means Mr. Cooney cannot be the Bugman!"

"It's all the Fritos," Willow told me solemnly. "They're destroying his brain."

Carl shoved another handful of Fritos in his mouth. "I'm right," he mumbled. "You'll see."

The next day I fooled around as long as I could at Mrs. Lowy's. I watered the front and back lawn and did some trimming and weeding.

But I had to go over to Mr. Cooney's. He's not the Bugman, I told myself. The Bugman is dead— if there every really was a Bugman in the first place.

"Janet," Mr. Cooney called from the porch as soon as I started across his front lawn. "I got out the gardening tools for you."

I hope they're in better shape than his lawn mower, I thought. I hurried over and grabbed the tools off the porch railing.

"Have some juice before you start," Mr. Cooney said.

"No, thanks," I answered. "Mrs. Lowy just gave me a big glass of lemonade."

I turned toward the front flower bed. Mr. Cooney wasn't the Bugman. But that didn't mean I wanted

44

to spend the morning sitting on the porch with him—especially after I saw him kiss that awful, ugly tarantula.

"I made this batch for *you*," Mr. Cooney said. I heard him climbing down the porch steps.

I sighed. Then I forced myself to smile as I turned back to him. "I'm really not thirsty," I said. "Thanks, anyway."

Mr. Cooney held a tall glass of the juice out toward me. "Drink it, Janet." His tone was sharp. And his wet black eyes gleamed behind the thick lenses of his glasses.

What is his problem? I wondered.

"Take it," he said again, his voice high and angry. "You must drink it."

No way am I drinking that stuff now, I thought. I took the glass from Mr. Cooney—and let it slip through my fingers. It shattered on the stone walkway.

"Oh, I'm so sorry!" I exclaimed. I hoped I sounded sincere.

"I'm such a klutz."

Mr. Cooney turned without a word. He marched back into the house.

He's furious at me, I thought. But I didn't care.

I bent down to pick up the pieces of broken glass.

Hundreds of tiny bugs came out of nowhere. They

45

surrounded the puddle of green juice. Hundreds. Thousands of bugs.

Sucking up the juice.

I kneeled down to get a closer look. As I watched, their bodies started to swell. To grow.

The bugs were doubling . . . no, tripling in size.

8

I stared down at the circle of insects.

What is going on here? I thought. What is in that juice? I drank that juice. *What is it doing to me?*

The screen door opened and slammed shut.

I saw Mr. Cooney rushing down the porch steps. Another big glass of the juice in his hand.

"Don't worry about spilling it," he said. "Plenty more where that came from."

I glanced down at the bugs again. They fought for the remaining juice. Their bodies still expanding.

A cricket swelled up. Growing rounder and rounder. Bigger and bigger. It sucked up more juice.

More juice—bigger and bigger.

Then *pop*. It exploded. Green goo spewed out everywhere. The other bugs swarmed around the cricket—and drank the liquid draining out of its body.

"Take the juice, Janet," Mr. Cooney whispered. "Take it."

"No!" I cried. "There's something horrible in that juice. I don't want it."

I turned and ran. Bugs crunching and squishing under my sneakers. Coating the bottoms with green slime.

"Janet!" Mr. Cooney yelled.

I didn't look back. I kept running. Running. Running.

The pool. I'll go to the pool. I'll relax. I'll think about what to do. Maybe Willow will show up. I can talk to her about this.

My side started to ache. I started to wheeze. But I didn't stop running until I reached the wire fence around the pool.

No Willow. Maybe she's in the locker room, I thought. I went over to the locker room.

I stared around. The locker room was almost empty. Just a mom trying to get her little girl to put on a pair of flip-flops.

Okay, I told myself. Calm down. You're safe now.

48

"What's wrong with her?" I heard the little girl ask. Her mother shushed her as they walked out.

I dropped down on one of the wooden benches and leaned forward. Trying to catch my breath.

That's when I saw it.

The scab on my knee. Shiny purple-black. About the size of a quarter—but thicker.

How did I get that? When did I hurt my knee?

I poked the scab with my finger. It felt hard. Hard and *crunchy*.

I jabbed the scab again. It cracked open . . . and oily green liquid oozed out.

Green liquid. Like Mr. Cooney's juice. My stomach lurched.

I closed my eyes and saw the cricket exploding again. Spraying green goo.

"No," I whispered. This can't have anything to do with the juice.

But it did. I knew it did.

I jumped up and rushed to the bathroom. I propped my knee up on one of the sinks and splashed it with hot water. As hot as I could stand.

Then I soaked a paper towel and covered it with the pink soap from the dispenser.

I scrubbed the scab. Scrubbed and scrubbed with the gritty soap. But it didn't come off.

The paper towel fell apart. I grabbed another one,

49

covered it with soap, and attacked the scab again. I had to get it off me. I had to.

This isn't working, I thought. I tossed the paper towel in the trash and started digging at the scab with my fingernails. Finally it popped off and fell into the sink.

I let my breath out with a *whoosh*. Then I ran hot water over my knee until the skin turned bright red and wrinkly.

I snapped off the water, eased my knee off the sink, and sat down on the tile floor.

I couldn't stop shivering.

Mr. Cooney's green juice did this to me, I thought. I know it. And that means . . . that means that Mr. Cooney could be the Bugman.

I slowly climbed to my feet.

I *knew* what I had to do.

I had to find out the truth about Mr. Cooney— and that green juice he kept feeding me.

I had to go back to his house.

After dark. It had to be after dark. I didn't want to get caught.

50

9

~~≈~~

I stared across the dark street at Mr. Cooney's
house. I'll have to get closer than this, I thought. A
lot closer if I want to find out the truth about Mr.
Cooney—and that disgusting green juice of his.

Okay, I decided. I'll count to three. Then I'll run
over to the big pine tree in his front yard.

One. Two. Three.

I pounded across the street and pressed myself
against the trunk of the tall tree. The bark felt rough
against my cheek.

I peered around the tree trunk at the big old

house. No lights came on. I didn't hear footsteps or the sound of a door opening.

Safe. So far.

I wish Willow were here, I thought. Or even Carl.

But Willow never showed up at the pool. I didn't have her phone number or anything, so I couldn't tell her my plan.

And Carl was up in my room right now—playing tapes, eating cookies, and talking to himself. Mom and Dad thought I was up there with him. They would never suspect I slipped out while they sat watching TV.

Stop stalling, I ordered myself. Okay, now I'll count to three and climb the fence into the backyard.

I figured I'd have better luck in the back of the house. That's where I found Mr. Cooney kissing his tarantula.

One. Two. Three.

I dashed to the wooden fence and hauled myself to the top. Splinters dug into my palms. The fence groaned and creaked, shaking underneath me.

I jumped down into the backyard—and froze where I landed. Crouched down as low to the ground as possible.

Did he hear me?

I didn't move. My legs started to cramp. Worse than when our P.E. teacher Ms. Mason makes us do a million deep knee bends.

52

A dog barked, and I heard a guy yelling for it to shut up. Other than that, the neighborhood was still and quiet.

I circled around the house. Walking with my knees bent so I would be harder to see from the house. Almost there, I told myself. Almost there.

I pushed through the bushes that grew below the windows and strained to see inside. Too high. I stretched up onto my tiptoes—but still couldn't quite see inside. I needed something to stand on.

I glanced around the backyard. That plastic garbage can would probably work, I decided. I hope it's empty.

I squeezed back through the bushes and hurried over to the can. Good—empty. I pulled it underneath the window and flipped it over. Then I climbed on top.

The heavy plastic buckled under my weight. But the garbage can didn't collapse. Whew!

I rose up on my knees and peered into the window. I saw a big room glowing with a dim blue light.

I leaned into the room, bracing myself on the window ledge. Good thing Mr. Cooney loves bugs so much, I thought. I don't have to worry about window screens.

Tables filled the room. And on the tables stood row after row of huge glass tanks. That's where the light is coming from, I realized. The tanks.

53

I needed to see more. I had to go inside.

I took a deep breath and swung one leg into the room. The garbage can flew out from under me and landed with a *thud*.

He had to hear that, I thought. Should I run? No, I needed to keep going. I pulled my other leg inside and dropped to the floor.

I lifted my head—and stared straight into a tank of cockroaches. Their shiny brown bodies glistening as they climbed over a hunk of rotting meat.

I pushed myself to my feet and glanced down into the next tank. Centipedes. Thousands of them. I could hear a soft rustling sound as they crawled over one another, their antennae waving wildly. Gross.

The next tank held a brown and white rabbit. It stared up at me, its little pink nose twitching. What are you doing in here, little bunny? I thought.

The rabbit hopped toward its food bowl. And I saw the fat gray leech clinging to its stomach.

I squeezed my eyes shut for a moment. Then I opened them and forced myself to keep moving.

I felt as if I were in a maze. The tanks of insects forming hallways and corridors.

I was surrounded by bugs. Thousands and thousands of them. My skin started to itch. I could almost feel all those little legs scurrying over me.

I have to get out of here. Now, now, now. Looking at all these bugs isn't going to help me.

I wove through the rows of tanks. Rushing faster and faster. Trying to find my way to the door. Then I turned a sharp corner. What I saw made my heart give a hard thump against my rib cage.

Mr. Cooney sat hunched over an old-fashioned desk only a few feet from me. His back was turned, and he appeared absorbed in the papers in front of him.

I inched away from him. Quietly, so quietly. I didn't want to think about what he would do if he caught me spying on him.

I took a few more small steps back.

Mr. Cooney straightened up.

Did he hear me?

Mr. Cooney reached up toward the bookshelf over the desk.

Close, I thought. I glanced over at him again—and almost screamed.

Something was wrong with Mr. Cooney. Horribly wrong!

He didn't have a hand on the end of his arm.

He had a claw. An enormous claw. Sharp and gleaming.

Like the pincer of a giant bug!

55

10

Mr. Cooney stretched open his pincer and clamped down on a book.

He doesn't have hands. He's not human. Mr. Cooney is part bug!

It's the Bugman. Mr. Cooney *is* the Bugman!

I spun around—and slammed into one of the glass tanks.

I lunged for it. But I wasn't fast enough.

The tank crashed to the floor—exploding into a million shards of glass.

Tiny white maggots flew across the room. One hit

me in the forehead. It rolled down my cheek and dropped onto the floor.

"Babies!" Mr. Cooney shrieked. Then he saw me. "What have you done to my babies?"

I turned to face him. "I . . . I'm really, really sorry, Mr. Cooney. I didn't mean to. I just bumped into the tank, and, and . . ." I stammered. "I'll work it off, I promise."

"You think you can *pay* me, and my babies will be all right?" he screeched in fury. He pointed at the floor with his horrible pincer.

I stared down at the hundreds of maggots. Blindly crawling over the sharp glass.

"You hurt them!" Mr. Cooney exploded. He glared at me through his thick glasses. "Some of them might even be dead!"

"I'm sorry," I repeated. "I'm so, so sorry."

"Sorry," Mr. Cooney snarled. "Sorry." He stalked toward me, the broken glass crunching under his feet. "My babies are dead and you're *sorry?*"

Mr. Cooney reached up and tore off his thick glasses. Ragged pieces of skin pulled away with them. His nose fell onto the floor with a moist *plop!*

I screamed. Screamed until my throat felt raw.

Mr. Cooney grabbed a strip of skin from his forehead and yanked it away. He threw it down on the floor in front of my feet.

I clenched my teeth together to keep from screaming again. A low moan escaped my lips. I shook my head back and forth, back and forth.

He tore off his right ear. Ripped away his left. Oily green goo spattered across the floor.

Mr. Cooney gave a high squeal. He peeled away his lips.

A mask! His whole face is a mask, I realized.

Now I saw the real Mr. Cooney. The real *Bugman.*

He had the head of a giant fly. No nose. A sucker for a mouth. His skin covered with rough black bristles.

And his eyes. His eyes were the worst. They bulged away from his head. Wet and shiny.

They were divided into sections—like two enormous golf balls. I could see myself reflected over and over—in each part of his black eyes.

Mr. Cooney grabbed his floppy white hat and yanked it off. A long pair of antennas uncurled. One shot out and brushed against my cheek. It felt dry and rough.

Run, my mind ordered. Run!

But I couldn't. My legs wouldn't move. They felt rooted to the floor.

I couldn't look away from Mr. Cooney.

I heard a horrible moist sucking sound. I gazed around wildly. What is that?

I realized the sound came from Mr. Cooney's mouth.

He leaned closer toward me, his eyes glistening with anger.

And spat a stream of bright green liquid at me.

12

The green spit splattered across my bare arm. Bubbling and foaming until it soaked into my skin.

My skin turned dead white. And cold. Cold clear through to the bone. So cold it burned.

I heard Mr. Cooney making that sucking sound again. He's getting ready to spit! I realized.

I jumped back. I grabbed the closest tank and heaved it off the table. It shattered on the floor between me and Mr. Cooney. Pieces of glass flew across the room.

Hundreds of red ants poured out of the tank. The biggest ants I had ever seen.

Mr. Cooney shrieked in agony. He lunged toward me—his pincer clicking open and shut.

I dived under the nearest table—grinding the ants under my hands and knees. Their bites felt like hot needles jabbing into my skin, but I didn't stop. I couldn't stop.

I crawled out the other side and shoved the table over. Two more tanks crashed to the floor. I heard a furious buzzing, but I didn't look back to find out which insects I had released.

I dashed for the window. Stumbling as I followed the twists and turns of the maze of tanks.

I heard Mr. Cooney crooning to his *babies*. Then I heard him coming after me. His pincer snapping open and shut. *Click, click, click.*

I leaped for the windowsill and hauled myself on top. I wriggled through the opening on my stomach. I could see the backyard. See the grass and the trees and the lawn. Almost there. Almost there, I thought.

I pushed off with both hands—and something grabbed my foot. Squeezing it tighter and tighter. I twisted around and stared over my shoulder.

I saw Mr. Cooney's pincer locked around my ankle. "You're not going anywhere!" he shouted.

I kicked frantically. Tried to squirm away. Then I reached out of the window as far as I could and grabbed one of the bushes with both hands.

I pulled myself toward the bush. Fighting to hold on to the tiny branches.

Mr. Cooney yanked on my foot—hard. I almost lost my grip. He yanked again.

My shoe popped off in his pincer, and I fell face first into the bush.

I jumped up and ran. Raced around the house, over the fence, across the front lawn.

Is he following me? I didn't stop to check.

Tiny stones dug through my sock and into my foot. But I couldn't stop. Didn't stop until I reached my front door.

I pulled open the door and stumbled into the hallway. "Mom," I croaked. My throat too dry to yell. "Mom!" I tried again.

The room whirled around me. I felt dizzy, so dizzy. I couldn't stand up. I collapsed on the hard floor of the front hall.

My eyes drifted shut. I knew I should try to yell for help. But I felt too weak, too woozy.

I felt a cold hand on my forehead.

"Janet!" a voice called. It sounded so far away. "Janet, what's wrong?"

I forced my eyes halfway open. Mom!

"Is she okay?" someone else asked. I thought it was Carl.

"Mom," I mumbled. "Bugman's after me. He spit on me. I spilled his maggots . . . I mean his babies.

He likes to call them his babies. Didn't mean to, Mom."

My eyes fluttered shut again. I couldn't hold them open a moment longer.

"You're burning up," I heard Mom say. She sounded even farther away now. "You have a fever. But you're okay. . . . You're going to be okay. . . ."

I shook my head back and forth. I felt the floor rock beneath me. "No, no, no," I protested. "Don't understand. Don't understand, Mom. He pulled his *face* off. And he spit at me. And he's going to come after me."

"Herb!" Mom called in her teeny, tiny voice. Why did her voice sound so funny? "Herb, there's something wrong with Janet!"

I heard Dad running up. He touched my head with his big hand. "You're right. She's on fire."

"You go on home, Carl," Mom said. "I'll call your mother later."

"Dad," I begged. "You have to help me get away. The Bugman is coming. And he's so mad at me. I broke open his tombstone and then I hurt his babies. But I didn't mean to. I didn't mean to."

"It's like the time when she was six, remember?" Mom asked. I could hardly hear her. "She had a high fever and thought a man-eating plant was growing in her stomach."

"Let's get her to bed." I felt Dad scoop me up in his arms.

"I'm going to call the doctor," Mom answered.

All the colors in the room ran together, swirling around me. Swirling in front of my eyes. I couldn't see Mom and Dad anymore. But I knew Dad was carrying me up the stairs.

He put me down on the bed and pulled off my other shoe. The colors in front of my eyes faded. My head cleared a little.

That's when I saw it. On my arm. Right where the Bugman's spit landed.

A shiny purple-black scab about as big as my fist.

"No. No, no, no," I moaned.

I reached down and rubbed my fingers over the spot. It felt thick and hard. And *crunchy*.

Like the shell of a giant beetle.

13

"**D**ad, I'm turning into a bug. You've got to help me. Please." I struggled to sit up, but my dad pressed me back onto the bed.

"Shhh. Shhh," Dad coaxed. "You're safe, Janet. Nothing bad is going to happen to you. I'm right here."

I clawed at the big scab. I had to pull it off.

Dad caught both my hands in one of his. "Don't, Janet."

He doesn't understand, I thought. I have to make him understand.

I concentrated as hard as I could. Start at the

beginning, I thought. "Listen, please," I begged him. "I was mowing. *Mowing.* And I hit a tombstone— the Bugman's tombstone. And he's mad. He's so mad at me, Dad."

"No, no, Janet," Dad crooned. "He's not mad. Who could be mad at you?"

Mom rushed in and sat down on the bed next to me. I stared up at her. "Mom, I'm a bug. Dad doesn't understand. I'm a *bug.*"

"She's delirious," Dad said softly.

Mom slipped the thermometer under my tongue. "Don't talk now, Janet. We have to see how high your temperature is."

I opened my mouth to try and explain again. But my mom grabbed my chin lightly between her fingers. "You can't talk now. Keep still—only for a minute, okay?"

They're never going to believe me, I thought. Never.

"I called Dr. Walker," my mom told my dad. "She's out of town. I told her service it was an emergency, so the doctor who is covering for her is coming right over. He's supposed to be very good, too."

Doctor, I thought. Maybe a doctor could help me.

Mom pulled the thermometer out of my mouth. "A hundred and four," she said.

I lay still, focusing on what I needed to tell the doctor.

"Do you want some ice water, honey?" Mom asked.

I shook my head. I need to rest now, I thought. Rest so I can tell the doctor what the Bugman did to me. Maybe he can do tests on that green goo. That green goo in the scab.

I raised my arm and stared at the purple-black scab. "It's bigger," I whispered. "It's *growing.*"

"What, baby?" Mom asked.

I shook my head. "Nothing," I mumbled. I knew she wouldn't believe me. I lowered my arm back to my side.

I shivered. How long would it take for the scab to get so big it covered my whole arm? My whole *body?*

The doctor has to help me, I thought.

Mom pulled my extra comforter out of the closet and spread it over me. "You're shaking," she said.

The doorbell rang. "That should be the doctor," Mom told me.

"He'll fix you right up," Dad promised as we waited.

My door opened and Mom stepped back in. "Honey, this is Dr. Brock. He's not your usual doctor—but he's filling in for Dr. Walker until Dr. Walker is back from vacation."

I hope he'll listen to me, I thought. If he doesn't . . .

Mom led the doctor into the room.

I stared up at him. Baggy long-sleeved shirt. Long green pants.

He leaned toward me. Peering at me through thick, thick glasses. His black eyes glittering.

"Noooo!" I yelled. "Get him away from me. He's the Bugman!"

14

~~~

The Bugman! He followed me.

"It's the Bugman!" I shouted. "I have to get out of here!"

I threw off the comforter and scrambled out of bed. But before I got halfway to the door, Dad grabbed my by the shoulders.

Dad wouldn't let go. He turned me around to face the Bugman. I opened my mouth to scream again.

Wait. Wait. It isn't the Bugman.

The doctor wore the same thick glasses. But the doctor had curly blond hair. He smiled at me gently.

"Janet, this is Dr. Brock, Dr. Brock," my mother repeated over and over.

I nodded. "I'm sorry," I mumbled. I felt like such an idiot. I returned to the bed and sat down.

"It's okay," Dr. Brock answered. "Most people with high fevers have some strange thoughts."

Oh, no! He'll never believe me now. He'll never believe that the Bugman has done something horrible to me!

Dr. Brock did all the usual stuff. Made me cough while he listened with the stethoscope. Used a little light to check my eyes. Looked in my ears and throat.

"Nothing serious," he told my parents. "I'll give you a prescription for some antibiotics. Janet will be fine in no time."

"What about this scab?" I blurted out. I held up my arm.

Dr. Brock turned to me. He ran his fingers over the huge purple-black scab.

I have to at least try and get him to help me, I thought. "This happened when the Bugman spit at me. The spit was bright green. It landed right there." I pointed to the scab.

"I'll get you an ointment for that," Dr. Brock told me. He glanced at my parents. "If it doesn't start clearing up in a few days, let me know."

70

"Please listen. Mom, Dad, make him listen," I begged. "Break open the scab. There is this green stuff in it. *Green.* Like the juice the Bugman gave me to drink."

I scratched the scab with both hands, trying to show them the oily green mucus. "You can do tests on it!" I cried.

My parents each grabbed one hand. "Calm down, sweetie. Calm down," Mom pleaded.

"This medicine should take the fever down," Dr. Brock said. "It may make her very sleepy, but right now she needs a lot of rest."

"No!" I protested. No, I can't sleep. I have to do something. The scab was growing. The Bugman was after me. If I went to sleep now . . .

Dr. Brock handed me two tiny pills. Mom gave me the glass of ice water from my bedside table.

I tried to swallow the water without swallowing the pills—but they started to dissolve in my mouth. They tasted so bitter I swallowed them before I could stop myself.

"Bye, Janet," Dr. Brock said. "Call me if the fever doesn't break," he added to my mom.

"We'll let you sleep now," my dad said. "We'll be right downstairs if you need us."

Okay, I thought as my parents and Dr. Brock left the room. I'll wait for a while, then I'll sneak out.

I yawned. I felt so tired. So sleepy.

I stretched out on the bed. I'll close my eyes, I thought. Just for a minute. Just for a minute.

When I opened my eyes, I couldn't see anything. Blackness surrounded me.

"Mom," I called. My mouth felt dry and gritty. "Mom?" I tried again. No answer.

The bed felt so hard. And cold.

I squinted, trying to see through the darkness. Tiny dots of light came into focus. Hundreds of dots of light.

Stars, I realized. Those are stars!

I'm outside!

How did I get out here? Did I sleepwalk?

I tried to sit up—but I couldn't. I couldn't move.

What is going on? I thought. What's happening to me now?

I fought to lift my head, the muscles in my neck straining. Then I stared down at my body.

A low moan escaped from my throat. My body . . . I was buried in mud up to my neck.

How did I get out here?

Who did this to me?

"Mom!" I yelled. But my throat was too dry to make much sound. She would never hear me from all the way down here.

72

I struggled to sit up again. But the mud was packed tightly around me.

No, not just mud, I realized. A mix of mud and leaves and twigs that formed a shell around me.

No! Not a shell.

A *cocoon!*

15

~~~

I pulled my hands out of the muddy cocoon and started to pull the leaves and twigs off me. As I did, parts of a dream came back to me. I saw myself climbing out of bed—walking to this tree and working to build this cocoon. But it wasn't a dream. It was real. I made this cocoon because I'm turning into a bug.

The Bugman is turning me into a huge bug. I'll end up exactly like him.

"Noooo," I wailed. "No, I don't want to be a bug!" I had to stop him. Somehow I had to stop him.

I struggled to kick my feet and break through the shell. I could only get my toes to move a few inches.

I dug harder with my hands, tearing at the mud on my legs.

Hurry, hurry, hurry, I ordered myself. I didn't know how much time I had. How long would the transformation take? How long would I still be human?

I wriggled and kicked until my legs broke free.

Then I scrambled up. I was covered with leaves and twigs and grass and mud. I brushed off as much as I could. I touched my arms and legs searching for more of those horrible scabs. But the mud was too thick.

I tiptoed to the back door and opened it as quietly as I could. I didn't want Mom or Dad to see me like this. They wouldn't believe me. They would get the doctor back here in a second.

I didn't turn on the lights. I crept through the kitchen and down the stairs to the basement. I washed up at the big sink.

The scab on my arm was a little bigger. But I didn't see any other changes. At least not yet.

I put on clean clothes from the laundry basket and rolled the muddy ones into a little ball. I stuffed them behind the dryer. I'd figure out what to do with them later.

I had no time now. All that mattered was getting to the Bugman.

I reached the kitchen door. It swung open before I could grab the doorknob.

"Janet!" my mom exclaimed. "What are you doing down there? I went into your room to check on you and you were gone."

Oh, no! Now what am I going to do? I didn't have one second to waste.

"Um, I guess I was sleepwalking," I told her. "I'll just go back up to bed." I tried to rush past her.

"That happened when you were nine and had a fever," Mom answered. She followed right behind me. "I'll sit with you until you fall asleep."

I'm doomed. Doomed, I thought. There is no way out of this.

I had no choice. I followed Mom upstairs.

Tap. Tap. Tap.

Mom poked her head in the door. "You had a good sleep," she said. She hurried over and pressed her hand on my forehead. "And your fever is down."

"I feel fine," I answered. I swung my legs off the bed. I had to convince Mom to let me outside.

"Not so fast," she said. "You're going to spend the day in bed. But your friend Willow is downstairs if you feel well enough to see her."

"Willow? Yes! I want to see her. Please," I said in a rush.

"For a short visit," Mom answered. "You're not over this virus yet." She headed downstairs. A few minutes later Willow peeked into my room.

"Come inside and close the door," I ordered her. "I have something really important to tell you."

Willow rushed over and sat down on my bed. "Your mom said you were really sick," she said.

"The Bugman is doing something horrible to me," I began. "I think he's turning me into a bug. You've got to help me."

Willow tried to smile. But she looked worried.

"Oh—my mother must have told you I would say that," I said. "She thinks my fever made me delirious or something. But it didn't. And anyway I feel fine now."

I took a big breath and hurried on. "I went to the Bugman's house yesterday—"

"What?" Willow interrupted.

"I had to," I answered. "I had to try and find a way to stop him."

"Wait, wait. Slow down," Willow protested. "What happened after I saw you that day with the tarantula?"

"I went to Mr. Cooney's the next day. He wanted me to drink more of this green juice he makes—he's been giving it to me every day since I met him. I wouldn't. I dropped the glass on the ground. All these bugs started drinking it—and getting bigger and bigger."

"But—" Willow began.

"Let me finish," I said. I could tell Willow was ready to interrupt again. I talked faster and faster so she wouldn't have a chance. I needed to tell her everything before my mom came back upstairs.

"Last night he caught me spying on him—and he ripped his face right off," I continued. "His human face was a mask. He really has the head of a giant fly or something."

"Whoa," Willow whispered. She hesitated. "Janet, don't get mad, okay? Couldn't your mom be right? Couldn't you have imagined the whole thing?"

"No way!"

Willow held up her hand. "Listen. When you're sick you can have some really weird dreams, even visions. I remember when I—"

"It wasn't a dream!" I insisted. *"Or* a vision. It wasn't.

"You've got to help me figure out a way to get back over to the Bugman's house. My mom will hardly let me out of her sight. But if I don't figure out what he's doing to me—I won't be able to stop him."

"Okay, okay," Willow said softly. "I believe you."

Willow thought for a minute. "I'll go for you," she

said. "It's the only way. We'd never be able to sneak you out past your mom."

"No. No, you can't go over there alone. It's too dangerous," I told her.

"I'll be careful. I'll look for evidence that he can turn people into bugs. And maybe I can get a sample of that juice," Willow said.

"I don't know," I said. "It's too scary. He really is a monster."

"Don't worry," Willow whispered. "I'll be careful. I'll go to his house right now. Don't worry. We'll find a way to stop the Bugman together."

"Thank you," I said. "Thank you so, so much. You're the best, Willow."

"I'll come back here as soon as I'm done," Willow promised. She jumped up and rushed out the door without looking back.

I climbed out of bed and stared down at the front yard. I watched Willow run out of the door and head toward Fear Street.

I rubbed my fingers over the scab on my arm. Bigger. Definitely bigger.

I watched Willow turn down Fear Street. Toward the Bugman's house.

Was she already too late?

16

I climbed back in bed and pulled my comforter up to my chin. Mom brought up some magazines, but I couldn't concentrate on reading. All I could think about was Willow.

I tried to picture every step she made—so I would know when to expect her back.

Okay. She left my room, walked down the stairs, said bye to my mom. Then put on her purple and yellow backpack, went out the front door, and ran down the street.

I could imagine everything Willow did—until she got to the Bugman's house. Then I couldn't come up with anything. I didn't know what would happen there.

And I couldn't do anything to help Willow. That was the worst.

I checked the clock. 11:14. Not even an hour since Willow left.

I asked Mom to bring the little TV from the kitchen upstairs. But even the wacko people on the talk shows couldn't hold my attention.

I checked the clock again. 1:00.

She should be back by now, I thought. I picked at the ragged skin around my thumbnail. She really should be back by now.

Maybe she had to wait for the Bugman to leave the room where his desk is. That could take a while.

Mom brought me up some lunch. I wasn't very hungry, but I ate some anyway. Then I tried to take a nap. But I couldn't fall asleep.

I rolled over onto my side and stared at my scab. Was it really bigger? Were there more of them? I couldn't tell anymore.

I looked at my alarm clock. Watching the seconds and minutes change. Waiting for Willow.

2:00. 3:00. 4:00. 5:00. No Willow.

Maybe I should call Carl and ask him to look for her. But the phone was downstairs. Mom might hear me.

Mom would think I was delirious again. I couldn't

risk her giving me another sleeping pill. I had to stay awake. I had to wait for Willow.

Dad came up to visit. I didn't feel like talking.

6:00. 7:00. 8:00. No Willow. And it would be dark soon.

I crawled out of bed and stared out the window. The street stood empty. What am I going to do if she doesn't come back?

9:00. 10:00. No Willow.

It was too dark to see anything out the window. I paced around my room. I felt too nervous to stay still.

Mom and Dad came in to say good night.

11:00. No Willow.

The Bugman has Willow!

Willow was trying to help me—and the Bugman got her. I knew it.

I'm sneaking out, I decided. I have to. I have to save Willow.

I pulled on jeans, sneakers, and a long-sleeved black T-shirt and started for my bedroom door. No. I couldn't risk going out the front way. I would have to walk right past Mom and Dad's bedroom—and one of them would hear me.

I opened my window and crawled out onto the garage roof. I slowly inched my way down to the edge and looked over. I grabbed the gutter and slid to the ground, holding on to the drainpipe.

I made it!

I took off for Fear Street. Please let me be in time, I thought. Please.

The Bugman's house stood dark and silent. I climbed over the back fence.

The garbage can. Where is it? I thought. I looked around. Then I saw something that made me gasp.

A piece of purple and yellow cloth rested on top of the Bugman's tombstone. It had to be Willow's. She always wore those colors.

I looked at the house. Still dark. I hurried over to the tombstone.

I grabbed the yellow and purple material. It's Willow's backpack, I realized.

Suddenly the ground rumbled and shook.

I fell onto the Bugman's tombstone.

What's happening? I thought. An earthquake?

Craaack!

The tombstone broke in half. The earth underneath it began to crumble.

A pit opened up. The two big pieces of granite started to slide into the pit.

I threw myself off the stone. Digging my fingers into the grass and weeds. Holding on, desperately clutching at the ground. Tearing at the dirt. Grabbing anything to keep from falling into the pit.

The earth bucked and shook. But I hung on—my legs dangling over the gaping pit.

83

Then the ground stopped shaking.

Still. Quiet. I crawled away from the pit—scraping my knees on stones and twigs.

Something sharp clamped around my ankle. It tore through the leg of my jeans.

I twisted around. "Noooo!" I shrieked.

The Bugman. He jerked on my ankle, pulling me down.

Down into his grave!

"Stop!" I screamed. "Let me go!"

The Bugman tightened his grip on my foot and yanked it hard.

I couldn't hold on. I slid into the grave. Down. Down. Down.

The earth rumbled, closing in around me. I couldn't see. My mouth and nose filled with dirt.

I couldn't breathe. My lungs ached and burned.

Then I was falling. Falling through the air.

Thunk!

I landed at the bottom of the grave. I sat up, coughing and choking.

I heard a sound behind me. I jumped up and turned around fast. The Bugman stood there watching me.

A whimper escaped from my throat. For the first time I saw the Bugman's true form. I couldn't stop staring at him.

His back . . . his back was covered by a shiny purple-black shell. The same color as the scab on my arm!

His legs were as skinny as broom handles.

And he had four arms. Two arms the regular human size and shape. And two shorter, thinner arms growing out of the center of his chest.

Each arm ended in a sharp pincer. The Bugman clicked them open and shut as he studied me with his enormous eyes. *Click! Click! Click! Click!*

"Come with me," the Bugman ordered in his high voice. He grabbed my wrist in his pincer. Then he pulled me through a narrow dirt tunnel.

We entered a large chamber—bigger than the first—filled with a strange yellow glow.

Where is that light coming from? I knew we were still underground.

Lightning bugs! Lightning bugs are giving the light, I realized. They clung to the sides of the hollowed-out room. Thousands of them, blinking on and off in different rhythms.

"Hello, hello, my dears," the Bugman crooned. He

released my wrist and scuttled over to the wall. "My sweet darlings," he called to the lightning bugs.

"I told everyone about you!" I shouted. "They will come looking for me—so you better let me out of here right now!"

The Bugman gave a high, shrill shriek. He spun toward me. I felt his hot breath hit my face. It smelled like rotting lettuce.

Then I heard a sucking, slurping sound. He's going to spit on me again! I covered my face with my arms and backed away from him.

"Janet!"

I recognized the voice at once!

"Willow? Where are you?" I stared around the large room.

"I'm here. On the floor."

Then I saw her. Wrapped in a cocoon from her neck to her feet.

I dashed over to her and kneeled down next to her. "The Bugman got you, too! Are you okay?"

She looked past me and smiled. "See? I *told* you she would come, Father!"

18

Father?

"No. No, Willow!" I cried. "The Bugman can't be your father. He must have given you something to make you believe that."

I grabbed the top of Willow's cocoon. "I'm tearing you out of there!" I yelled.

"Janet, don't!" Willow shouted. "You'll hurt me!"

The Bugman grabbed me by the back of my shirt and threw me against the wall. Then he came toward me. *Click! Click! Click! Click!*

"No, Father!" Willow exclaimed. "Don't hurt her! She's my friend. I want her for my friend."

The Bugman stared at me with his enormous black eyes. "I want you to be my Willow's friend, Janet. I won't hurt you—as long as you don't hurt Willow or the babies."

He really is her father, I realized. Willow tricked me. She planned to get me here all along!

"Why did you do this to me?" I yelled at Willow.

The Bugman began to hum. A high, whining sound.

How will I ever get out of here? What am I going to do? Mom and Dad don't know where I went. Maybe there's a way.

"I wanted you to be my friend," Willow said.

She sounded hurt. I couldn't believe it.

"You've got to listen to me. Please," Willow begged.

The Bugman pointed at her with one sharp pincer. Silently ordering me over to her.

I'll go along with them for a while, I decided. Until I can figure out what to do. I shuffled back over to Willow and sat down next to her cocoon.

"Okay. I'm listening. What?" I asked.

"I needed a friend. And I picked you," Willow answered. I noticed her green eyes glistening with tears.

"We *are* friends," I protested. I didn't want to

89

make Willow—or her father—upset again. Not until I found a way out of there.

"You don't understand," she said. "You can't really be my friend. Not the way you are. No one can."

I took a quick peek at the Bugman. He stood only a few feet behind me.

"Why not?" I asked.

"Because I'm only human part of the time. For two years I'm a girl. Then I go into a cocoon and spend two years as—"

"As a *bug?*" I interrupted. My stomach turned over.

"Yes. And it's so lonely. I make new friends. And then I lose them." Willow smiled up at me. "But now Father figured out a way to change you, too. Now we can be friends forever. Isn't that great?"

Great? She's nuts, I thought.

"I don't want to be a bug, Willow," I explained.

"Oh, you'll love it! You get to live in two worlds this way," Willow said. "You really feel part of the great circle of life. It's awesome!"

"But what about my family?" I asked. "I'll miss them."

"Father and I will be your family," Willow reassured me.

What could I say now? "But . . . but your father hates me. I destroyed his tombstone. I woke him from the dead."

Hmmm. Hmmm. Hmmm. The Bugman had started his humming again. But it sounded different. Lower. Not so piercing.

I glanced back at him. He rocked back and forth on his thin, thin legs, rubbing his pincers together. *Hmmm. Hmmm. Hmmm.*

The Bugman is laughing! I realized.

"What's so funny?" I asked.

"I was never dead," he answered in his high voice. "I was hibernating. A trick I learned from the seven-year locusts."

"But what about the tombstone?" I asked.

"Some boys put it there," the Bugman told me. "They became frightened of me once I began experimenting on myself. They didn't understand the thrill of transformation—of becoming half bug and half human."

The Bugman shook his head. "A group of them took me from my home and buried me in the yard," he continued. He began to click his pincers open and shut. "They thought I was dead. They put the tombstone on top of me."

He made his laughing-humming sound again. "But I wasn't dead. I was hibernating."

I swallowed hard. The Bugman could never be destroyed! I was trapped.

"See, Janet?" Willow said. "We'll be giving you a great new life. You'll live hundreds more years than most people."

"Thank you. I appreciate it, really," I told the Bugman. Then I turned my gaze to Willow. "But please choose someone else. I know it doesn't make sense to you, but I want to stay human."

"It's too late for that," the Bugman said. "The process has already begun."

My heart pounded so loud I could hardly hear him. "What?" I cried.

The Bugman scurried over to the dirt wall behind Willow. "Excuse me, babies," he said. He gently shooed some of the fireflies away.

Now I could see a small hole dug into the wall. A pitcher sat inside it. The same pitcher the Bugman used to serve the green juice.

Then I understood. "I was right!" I yelled. I jumped to my feet. "That juice you kept giving me— and the health shake Willow made—it's already started turning me into a bug."

"Yes," the Bugman answered. He picked up the pitcher and started toward me. "Now, have some more."

"No!" I shouted.

"Please, Janet. Be reasonable," the Bugman said.

"Never! Let me out of here!"

"Very well," the Bugman said firmly. "Babies! Do your work!"

19

Hundreds of bugs swarmed through the earth and came toward me. Beetles. Ants. Centipedes.

Something soft brushed against my face. Soft and sticky. I looked up. "No," I whispered.

A fat gray spider hung on a shiny thread in front of my nose. Another spider slithered down. Faster and faster, they dropped their threads around me.

I slashed my hand across the threads, and the spiders fell to the ground. More spiders slid down to take their place.

My ankles started to itch and burn. I stared down.

The cuffs of my jeans bulged as the army of bugs shoved their way inside.

I shook one leg, then the other. Bugs tumbled back onto the ground. But more kept coming.

Then I heard buzzing—getting louder and louder. I squeezed my eyes shut. I didn't want to see the wasps and bees arrive.

"Willow!" I screamed. "Help me! Please!"

Bugs flew into my mouth. I choked, coughing and spitting.

"It will be okay, Janet," Willow called. "Don't fight it. Let them build the cocoon. It's the final stage."

Cocoon? They're building a cocoon?

I opened my eyes. Every inch of my body was covered with bugs.

I tried to knock them off. But I couldn't. My arms were pinned to my sides.

The spiders are spinning webs around me, I realized. That's why I can't move.

A row of ants climbed onto my face. Each carried tiny twigs and pieces of leaves. They stuck to my skin.

The bees and wasps dive-bombed me. Dropping more leaves and bits of wax and honey.

Then all the insects turned and swarmed away from me. Burrowing into the soil. Climbing back into the ceiling. Flying out the tunnel.

"It's almost over," Willow called.

Almost?

The earth moved again. And rows and rows of thick yellow slugs burst through. They slithered toward me, and then crept up my body.

Their cold slime trails sealed the cocoon even more tightly.

I couldn't move at all.

The Bugman's babies had finished their work. They slid off me and disappeared.

"Time to sleep now," the Bugman announced in a singsong voice. He scurried over to Willow with the pitcher of green juice. He bent down and poured some into her mouth.

"See you when we wake up, Janet!" Willow cried. "Just think of this as a slumber party—with our cocoons as sleeping bags."

"Willow, no. Tell your father you changed your mind," I pleaded.

But she didn't answer.

The Bugman kissed Willow on the forehead. "Good night, Princess," he said.

"Good night, Father," she said. The Bugman placed a loose hood over her head. It looked as if it were made of spiderwebs.

Then the Bugman turned to me.

"No," I begged. "Please don't do this. Please. I

96

want to go home to my family. I want to stay human."

The Bugman shook his head. "It will all be over soon," he said. He pressed the pitcher of juice against my lips.

20

I twisted my head back and forth violently. I couldn't drink that juice.

The Bugman uttered a high, angry whine. He trapped my head between two of his pincers and forced the spout of the pitcher between my lips.

"Drink!" he ordered.

I clenched my teeth. Clenched them until my jaws ached.

Then the Bugman clamped my nose closed with one pincer. I couldn't breathe.

My chest started to burn. But I didn't open my

mouth. My heart thudded harder and harder. But I kept my teeth locked together.

Air, I thought. I need air.

Tiny red dots burst in front of my eyes.

I had to have air.

I opened my mouth and sucked in a big breath.

I tried to slam my teeth shut again. Too slow. The Bugman tilted back my head and poured the green juice into my mouth.

No! I won't drink it, I thought.

I spit it out—aiming for the Bugman's black eyes.

He squealed in pain. Got him!

The Bugman dropped the pitcher onto the ground and stumbled away from me. He scrubbed at his eyes with all four pincers.

"You are not worthy of being my daughter's friend!" the Bugman screamed. His antennae whipped back and forth. Green drool dripped from his mouth. He began snapping all four pincers open and closed.

I wiggled and squirmed, trying to break free of the cocoon. But the webbing was too tight. My arms stayed glued to my sides. And my feet were locked together.

"I was going to give you a beautiful life—but you're not worthy!" the Bugman shrieked. "Now you must be *exterminated!*"

21

The Bugman charged at me.

I threw my weight forward—and slammed into him. We both fell.

I rolled over and over, still trapped in my tight cocoon. Then I thudded to a stop against the crumbly dirt wall.

The Bugman gave a shrill squeal.

He's coming after me, I thought. And I can't even stand up.

I twisted my neck around. Where is he?

Then I saw him. He lay flat on his big purple-black shell. All four arms and his skinny legs waved wildly in the air.

He can't stand up! I knocked him over. He landed on his back—and he can't flip himself back over.

"Babies!" the Bugman cried. "Babies, help me. Help me."

All the bugs swarmed back up from the floor and walls and ceiling. Thousands of them. They crawled over the Bugman.

What if they are strong enough to help him up? I had to get out of the cocoon. Fast.

I rolled back and forth, struggling to break free of the webbing. But the cocoon didn't feel any looser.

I grabbed hold of the webbing under my chin the only way I could. With my teeth.

I gave it a yank—and a piece ripped off. I spit it out and bit into another section, the leaves and twigs crunching in my mouth. Gross!

I tore away as much of the webbing as I could reach. The cocoon felt looser now, and I could move one arm a little.

I glanced over at the Bugman. I couldn't see him at all. The insects covered him completely.

Hurry, I ordered myself. If his babies flip him right side up, you're dead.

I worked my arm back and forth until it burst free. I tore at the cocoon until I could use my other arm, too. Faster, faster, I thought.

I ripped a big piece of webbing off my legs and then kicked my way out of the bottom of the cocoon. I struggled to my feet and raced down the narrow tunnel.

I could still hear the Bugman screaming. Then I heard another voice. Willow's.

"Janet," Willow called. "Don't go! Don't you want to be my friend?"

I didn't answer. There is nothing I can do for her, I told myself. The tunnel split in two directions. One seemed to run uphill. I followed it, the dirt making me choke and cough.

The tunnel hit a dead end. I dug frantically, bringing down clumps of dirt on my head. Then I felt a cool breeze on my face—and saw the stars shining above me.

As I hauled myself through the hole I heard Willow's voice echo through the tunnel behind me. "Janet. Don't go. Stay. Don't you want to be my friend?"

Epilogue

~~~~~

*W*hap!

"Oww!" My back stung like crazy. I sat up and grabbed the beach towel out of Carl Beemer's hands. "You jerk!" I yelled.

Carl laughed and cannonballed into the pool, sending a tidal wave onto my notebook. He came up smirking.

"Jerk," I muttered again. Megan would be back tomorrow. And Anita and Sara would be home on Friday. I couldn't wait.

Carl swam over and rested his arms on the edge of

the pool. I held up my sopping notebook. "You got water all over my story," I snapped.

"You should change it anyway," Carl answered. I noticed he didn't bother to apologize. Typical.

"I think you should make me the hero," Carl continued. "I could run into the Bugman's lair and rescue you and Willow and get my picture in the paper."

"Yeah, right," I said. "As if you would do something that brave."

I smoothed the wrinkly pages of the notebook. "I just finished the end."

"Let's hear it," Carl said.

"'Nobody knew what happened to the Bugman or Willow after that,'" I read. "'They disappeared— and only the Bugman's big purple-black shell was ever found.

"'But what I cared about was that I was still *me*. Not a bug. Just a girl. A *human* girl. The End.'"

Carl snorted. He sounds like a hog when he does that. "Not bad," he admitted. "You might win that story contest in the paper. Since *I* didn't bother to write one myself."

He splashed some water in my face. "Yeah. It took a wild imagination to come up with a wacko story like that," Carl added. "What are you going to call it anyway?"

I thought for a minute. " 'The Bugman Lives!' " I announced.

I headed for home, my hair still wet from the pool. A beautiful purple and yellow butterfly fluttered around my head.

"Hey, I was hoping you'd come by the pool," I said.

The butterfly took off and landed near the top of the maple tree in the Hasslers' yard.

I rubbed my hands together. Sticky green mucus began oozing across my palms.

"I'll meet you up there," I called.

Slurp, slurp, slurp. I climbed straight up the trunk of the maple tree. This green stuff works better than suction cups, I thought.

The purple and yellow butterfly flew over and sat on my nose. I grinned at it. "I'm glad we're friends," I said. "I'd hate to spend the *whole* day with Carl."

The butterfly beat its wings together.

"I never could have climbed this high before I met you," I told the butterfly. "You were right, Willow. Some parts of being a bug *can* be awesome."

HALLOWEEN
BUGS ME!

Some kids are lucky.

Some aren't.

My name is Greg Dreamer. I'm smart. I'm a good athlete. And I'm a great drummer.

But I'm not lucky.

Don't get me wrong. I'm not complaining. Okay—maybe I am complaining.

But why can't *I* be lucky?

My friend Olivia is lucky.

Take today, for instance. Friday. Liv forgot to study for our math test. She was nervous. I could tell because she kept twirling her long brown braid around her fingers. That's what she does when she's nervous.

Anyway, we walked into class this morning and sat down at our desks. Liv was twirling away—when a substitute teacher walked into the room.

A substitute teacher! Can you believe it?

No math test.

That's lucky.

And that's what I was thinking as I walked home from school that afternoon and spotted Derek Boyd across the street.

Derek Boyd is the luckiest kid in the entire seventh grade. No—make that the luckiest kid in all of Shadyside Middle School.

Derek is always trying to prove he's better than me. He and I are always competing.

I have blond hair. But Derek's hair is blonder. I have blue eyes. But Derek's eyes are bluer.

I'm tall for my age—and strong. But Derek is taller and stronger. And he doesn't let me forget it.

Derek likes to compete. Derek likes to win. And he always does. *Always.* Like the last time we went on a class trip to the natural history museum. I found a quarter in the change return of the soda machine. Lucky, right?

But then I tried to buy a soda and the stupid machine ate all my money. Not just the quarter. All seventy cents.

Not so lucky.

And then Derek came along and bought a soda—

and the machine started spraying change at him like he hit the jackpot!

Now, that has to be luck. What else could it be?

If I were lucky, I could beat him. I know I could. That's what I was thinking when Derek walked over to me and burped in my ear. Really loud.

"Can you beat that, Dreamer?" He punched me in the arm. Really hard. I dropped my books on the sidewalk.

"Come on. I dare you. Try." He punched me again.

I glared at him. It was my I-mean-business look.

I took a deep breath. I gulped down some air.

I got ready to belch the loudest belch I could. This one would roar. I could feel it.

I opened my mouth—

"Hi, guys," Liv said. She tapped me on the back.

Broke my concentration.

I let out my burp.

It didn't quite roar.

"Got the hiccups again, Greg?" Liv asked.

"Ha! Hiccups! Good one!" Derek clapped me on the back. "Better luck next time."

Better luck next time. Yeah. Right.

"So—what are you going to be tonight?" Liv asked as I picked up my books.

It was Halloween. And I knew exactly what I was going to be. But I wasn't telling. I didn't want Derek to know. I didn't even want to give him a hint.

This Halloween I was finally going to beat Derek. This Halloween my costume was definitely going to be better than his.

"I'm not sure what I'm going to be," I lied.

"How about you, Liv?" Derek asked.

Liv hitched up her backpack. "My costume this year is totally great. I'm going as a mummy."

"Didn't you go as a mummy last year?" I asked.

"Yes. That's what's so great about it!" she exclaimed. "My costume is still in perfect condition. I don't have to waste time making a new one."

Liv is very into being practical.

Derek shrugged. "Well, I have a new costume, and it's awesome! It will definitely beat yours, Dreamer!" He punched me in the arm again. Then he took off down the block.

"He even runs faster than I do," I said, disgusted. "He beats me at everything."

"All this competing with Derek is crazy," Liv complained as we headed home. "Why do you do it?"

"Because I have to beat Derek at something," I told her. "I have to. Just once, I have to win."

Liv's house is on the same block as mine. The whole way home she went on and on about how stupid it was to compete.

"Stupid and crazy and sick. Stupid and crazy and sick," she said over and over again. "Stupid and crazy and—Uh-oh."

"Huh?"

"Uh-oh," Liv repeated. "Here comes Muffin."

I groaned. Muffin is Mrs. O'Connor's dog. My dad says Mrs. O'Connor is a nut. I don't know about that, but *Muffin* is definitely crazy. He's just a little Scottish terrier, but he thinks he's a Doberman.

The dog charged down the block, heading straight for us. *"Arf! Arf! Grrrf!"* he yapped.

"No!" I shouted as Muffin lunged for my right foot. He grabbed my shoelaces in his mouth. He tossed his head madly back and forth, tugging at them.

"Stop!" I ordered. But he just tugged harder, untying them. Chewing them to bits with his sharp teeth.

I handed my books to Liv. I pried Muffin's mouth open and freed my laces.

He growled—then sank his teeth into my other sneaker.

I knew from experience that Muffin wasn't going to quit. There was only one thing to do. "Come on!" I yelled to Liv. I started to run, dragging the dumb dog with me.

I dragged Muffin past two houses. Finally he had to let go. But then he chased me all the way to my front yard.

Liv and I leaped over my gate. We ran inside the house. I slammed the door behind us and collapsed on the hall floor.

5

"Greg, is that you?" Mom came out of the kitchen. She stared down at me. "Why are you sitting on the floor?"

"Because he's lazy," my six-year-old sister, Raina, piped up. She followed Mom out of the kitchen.

Liv choked back a laugh.

"Maybe you're right, honey." Mom ran her hand through Raina's curly blond hair. "Greg, you need exercise. Go up and clean your room. My book discussion group is coming tomorrow."

My mom is funny that way. I mean, why clean my room for her reading group? It's not like they're going to meet in *there*.

But try pointing that out to my mom.

"I'll clean it later, Mom. I want to show Liv something first."

"Greg, your room has to be clean before dinner. Otherwise . . . no trick-or-treating tonight," Mom warned.

"Okay, okay," I grumbled under my breath.

"What do you want to show me?" Liv asked as we headed up the stairs.

"You'll see."

"See what?" Raina asked, following us.

"Get lost," I told her.

"Greg! Don't talk to Raina that way," Mom yelled up the steps. "You're lucky to have a little sister who loves you."

Yeah. Lucky. Right.

Raina followed us right into my bedroom. She sat down on my rug. Our cat sauntered into the room and sat in her lap.

It was supposed to be *my* cat. I begged my mom and dad for it for months and months. "Raina has a hamster. Why can't I have a pet too?" I pleaded.

I knew just what I wanted. A mysterious, coal-black cat with deep green eyes. I'd seen him in the pet store.

My parents finally gave in and bought me a cat for my birthday. But they took *Raina* to the pet store with them. She got to pick out the cat. *And* name it.

I stared down at the cat.

Our sweet, small, white, fluffy cat with pale blue eyes.

Let me tell you something. A twelve-year-old guy should *not* have a sweet, small, white, fluffy cat. It's embarrassing.

Let me tell you something else. A twelve-year-old guy *definitely*—I repeat, *definitely*—should *not* have a cat named Princess.

"Boy, Princess really grew." Liv bent down to pet her.

"Yeah. But she's not as big as Derek's cat," I grumbled.

After we got Princess, Derek got a cat too. A really big cat. Coal-black with green eyes.

My cat.

"Greg, this dumb competition has got to end! It doesn't matter who has a bigger cat!" Liv shouted.

"It does matter!" I yelled back. "Derek always wins. But that's going to change. It's going to change today!"

"Today? Why today?" Liv asked.

"Because today is Halloween. And I'm going to show Derek this year who is best," I told her.

"And how are you going to do that?" Liv folded her arms.

"Simple," I answered. "I have a plan."

2

"Are you ready?" I called from inside my closet.

"I've been ready for the last ten minutes," Liv answered. "What are you doing in there?"

"You'll see. Just give me a few more seconds. It's all part of my plan," I said.

Then I leaped out of the closet—and Raina and Liv shrieked in terror.

"Wow! That's a great costume!" Liv reached out a hand and touched it. "Ewww. It's so . . . hairy."

"I know. Isn't it awesome?" I studied my costume in the mirror. My totally gruesome werewolf costume.

It was very hairy. Very thick and very hairy.

I had worked hard on that costume. I'd made it really gross. In some spots the fur was matted down

9

and sticky with a mixture of maple syrup and vegetable oil.

Dead bugs nested in the fur. Flies, worms—even a big, hairy spider. I must have spent two hours gluing them all in place. They were fake, but they looked pretty real.

"What's that?" Raina reached out. She touched a bloated worm clinging to the moist hair. "Oh, yuck!" She drew her hand back quickly. "It feels wet."

"Want to see something totally gross?" I asked.

I turned to show them the scab on the right side of the wolf mask. It looked like a fresh cut from a wolf fight. It had fake pus dripping from it and everything. It cost a lot extra. But I had to have it!

"It's a great costume, Greg." Liv couldn't stop staring at it. "It really is."

"I know." I took off the mask and smiled. "Derek is going to have to go pretty far to beat this. He's going to need more than a costume to beat *me* tonight. He's going to need a miracle!"

Liv sighed. Then she headed for the door.

"Hey! Where are you going? I'm not finished telling you the rest of my plan!"

She stopped in the doorway. "I'm going home. I think I've heard enough."

"Wait a second. Look!" I reached into my closet and pulled out a huge orange plastic trick-or-treat bag.

"Can you believe the size of this thing?" I asked her.

"It's ridiculous. It's as big as a suitcase!" Liv shook her head.

"I know. And tonight I'm going to fill it completely. I'm going to get twice as much candy as Derek!"

Liv started down the steps.

"Tonight is the night, Liv!" I called after her. "Tonight I am going to beat Derek. I'll have the best costume *and* the most candy!"

"Whatever," I heard Liz call. Then the front door slammed.

"Raina! Greg!" Mom called. "Come on down. Time for dinner."

"Will you give me some of your Halloween candy later?" Raina asked as we made our way downstairs.

"No way!" I scoffed.

"Then I'm telling Mom—" she started to whine.

"Mom won't care," I cut her off. "She doesn't want you to eat candy."

"I'm telling Mom," Raina started again, "that you didn't clean your room."

After dinner, I cleaned my room.

Then I went out to meet Liv.

In the light of the full moon, she was easy to spot. She was the only mummy wearing short-sleeved bandages.

"I forgot to check the sleeves," she said miserably. "My arms must have grown."

We walked a few steps. Then Liv stopped. She tried to tug her bandages down to her wrists.

I scanned the street, searching for Derek. Our block looks totally creepy tonight, I thought. Jack-o'-lanterns sat on almost every porch. Flickering candles inside them lit up their eerie grins and cast an orange glow over the houses.

A chilly breeze began to blow.

Something clattered behind us.

I spun around—and gasped. A skeleton hung from one of the branches. Its bones rattled in the wind.

The wind picked up. It howled through the trees. Leaves swirled at our feet.

I heard the distant laughter of some kids on the corner. But there was no sign of Derek.

We walked toward Mrs. O'Connor's house.

Liv stopped and tugged on her bandages some more.

"You look great. Really, Liv. Come on." I urged. "I want to find Derek. I can't wait to show him my costume. I can't wait to see his face."

We walked some more.

I heard rustling behind the tall bushes that lined the street.

I stopped and glanced around.

No one there.

We took a few more steps.

This time Liv heard the rustling too. Our eyes darted to the shrubs. We saw them quiver in the moonlight.

"Is someone following us?" Liv's voice shook.

"I—I think so," I whispered. "Walk faster."

We broke into a jog—and heard footsteps.

We started to run.

The footsteps grew louder. Closer.

The bushes to my left quaked, and a dark creature sprang out from them.

It was big. And hairy.

In the glow of the moon, I could see its red, burning eyes and its slack jaw gleaming with spittle.

"A werewolf!" I cried. "A real werewolf! Run, Liv!"

Before I could move, the werewolf let out a shuddering howl and leaped through the air!

3

The werewolf landed hard against my chest. Even through my mask I could smell its damp animal smell.

With its chest right against mine, it wrapped its heavy arms around me, locking my arms close to my sides. It bellowed a loud, deep growl.

I pushed my arms out. Hard. With a heave, I freed myself.

"Run, Liv! *Run!*" I cried again.

My heart pounding, I tore down the block.

"Did you see it?" I asked Liv, panting. "Did you see the werewolf? I—I think it had two heads!"

Liv didn't answer me.

I risked a glance to my right. Then my left.

14

Liv was nowhere in sight.

It's got her! I realized. *I have to go back! I have to help her!*

I spun around—and froze.

Liv stood right where I had left her—right next to the werewolf.

She stared at me for a second.

Then she burst into laughter.

"Oh no," I moaned. "It can't be. It just can't be!"

I made my way slowly back to Liv. I felt sick.

"You can run pretty fast—when you're scared to death!" the werewolf remarked. It took off one of its heads.

That's right. It was Derek—in a werewolf costume as gross as mine.

No—it was grosser.

The eyes on his mask glowed. And the fur was thicker. It even *smelled* like wolf fur.

The fake drool was really disgusting. And the costume had *two* heads. Two hideous heads.

"Not a bad costume." Derek ran his paw over my fur. "Like the bugs. Nice touch. But . . . I win!"

Now I was really steamed.

"See you." Derek started to leave. "It's time for me to collect more candy than you."

"No way!" I sputtered. *"I'm* the one who is going to collect the most candy. Look at this!" I held up my giant trick-or-treat bag. "There's no way I can loose with this."

"Whoa!" Derek stopped. His eyes opened wide. "That's a big bag!"

Then he grinned. "But it's not as big as mine!"

Derek held up his trick-or-treat bag. It was enormous. *Twice* the size of my bag.

My eyes narrowed. "I'll fill my bag up—and another and another!" I shouted.

"Dream on, Dreamer!" he hooted. "I'm going to win—because I always do!"

"Stop it!" Liv yelled. "Stop it, right now! This is sick. Who cares about stupid Halloween candy! Who cares about winning?"

"Gotta go." Grinning, Derek took off down the street.

"Come on, Liv." I tugged on her bandages, dragging her in the opposite direction from Derek. "We can't waste any time."

I charged blindly up to house after house. "Trick or treat!" I yelled as soon as anybody opened their door.

The second they dropped the candy in my bag, I was off, racing to the next house.

"Slow down," Liv complained.

"We can't slow down!" I panted. "We need more candy! Lots more candy!"

"Trick or treat! Trick or treat!"

I raced through the streets.

16

I think I rang nearly every doorbell in Shadyside. I collected candy. A lot of candy.

But it wasn't enough. When I glanced inside my bag, it was only half filled.

"Hurry, Liv! We need more!" I ran ahead and turned down the next block.

"Greg!" she cried. *"Stop!"*

I waited impatiently for her to catch up. "What's the matter?"

"Are you crazy? We can't trick-or-treat on this street!" she exclaimed.

"Why not?" I asked.

"Why not! You've totally lost it, Greg. Didn't you even notice where we are?" Liv pointed to the street sign. "We cannot trick-or-treat here. This is *Fear Street!*"

Fear Street.

I shivered in the cool October air.

Liv and I never walk down Fear Street. Never.

Too many weird things happen on this street. At least, that's what I've heard. I don't know whether to believe the stories or not, but Liv definitely does.

Liv says most of the houses on Fear Street are haunted. And horrible things happen in the ones that aren't.

She says she once met a kid who was trapped in the Fear Street Cemetery. Trapped by a ghost who wanted him to stay there. Forever.

17

And the Fear Street Woods—I shivered again just thinking about those woods. No birds live in the Fear Street Woods. None at all. And no one knows why.

Maybe Liv was right. Maybe we shouldn't . . .

No! We should!

Of course we should!

"Liv, we have to trick-or-treat on Fear Street!" I gripped her wrist. "Come on. It's perfect! Derek will never even think of trick-or-treating here! We'll clean up! We'll definitely get more candy than he will!"

Liv shook her head.

"Please, Liv? Just walk down the street with me. Please?"

"Oh, all right," she said at last.

I guided Liv down Fear Street. I walked slowly—because it was *really* dark. The streetlights are always out on Fear Street.

"We won't go to all the houses. Just a few. Nothing will happen to us. You'll see," I declared.

I sounded pretty convincing, I thought.

But as I gazed around, I started to change my mind.

Fear Street was definitely creepy.

The trees on our street were bright with red and yellow fall leaves. But the trees here were bare.

I gazed up at their branches. They grew thick and twisted tightly together. They hung low over our heads, blocking out even the slightest ray of moonlight.

The houses were even creepier.

They rose up high and sprawled out over the winding street. With their cold stone and brick, they sat dark and dreary. No colorful trim painted on the shutters. No cheerful welcome mats in front of the doors.

Rolling lawns stretched out in front of some of the houses—gardens of overgrown crabgrass, dotted with bald and blackened spots.

A high fence of rusted black iron ran next to the sidewalk. It was tipped with sharp spikes.

Another shiver ran through me.

Liv stared around and shivered too.

"I have a bad feeling about this, Greg," she murmured. She walked close to me.

"Everything is going to be fine," I told her as the wind began to gust.

"I don't think so." Liv reached for her braid. But it was tucked into her mummy costume. So she just grabbed a piece of bandage and started twisting that.

"Something is going to happen to us here," she said fearfully. "Something terrible. I just know it."

4

We stopped in front of a house near the end of Fear Street. A three-story house—a mansion, really.

I counted the windows. There were eight on each floor. Twenty-four windows! And that was just in the front.

Twenty-four windows—all totally dark. Not a glimmer of light peeked through. No lamp glow. No flicker from a TV or fireplace.

"Let's keep going," Liv said. "Nobody's home."

"Somebody might be home." I started up the dark path. "It's a big house. Maybe they're in the back."

Liv and I stepped up on the front porch. The old wood creaked under our weight. We stopped.

"Are you sure you want to do this?" Liv looped her loose bandages into a knot around her fingers.

I glanced up at the house. At the rotting shutters that dangled from the black windows. At the soot that caked the stone walls.

I wasn't sure at all.

I glanced up and down the block.

All the houses on Fear Street looked kind of spooky.

Might as well start with this one, I thought. *We have to start somewhere—and I* have *to get more candy than Derek!*

"We'll ring the bell, get our candy, and leave— fast," I promised.

I rang the bell.

We waited for someone to answer.

"Nobody's home. Let's go." Liv started to tug me down the steps. Then we heard the squeaky doorknob turn.

I turned around. The door opened a crack.

"Hello?" I called.

A green, scaly hand shot out from the dark and grabbed my wrist!

"Hey! Help! Let me go!" I yelled. I tried to jerk free, but the hand held on tightly.

"Let him go!" Liv smacked the hand hard.

We heard a cry inside.

A second later the hand released me . . . and the door swung open.

"Sorry." A boy stood in the doorway. He seemed about my age, but very thin, almost frail. His stringy dark hair hung in his eyes.

In his hand he held a fake monster claw. He waved it at us. "I was just trying to have some fun. It's Halloween, you know."

"Um, we know," I said. "We're trick-or-treating."

"Great," the boy said. "Come in. I'll give you some candy." He turned, motioning for us to follow.

"I am *not* going in there," Liv whispered to me.

"Come on. We'll go in for a second. We'll just get our candy and leave," I pleaded.

Liv rolled her eyes. But she followed me through the door.

We stepped inside. We stood in a large living room—in the glow of hundreds of flickering candles.

There were candles *everywhere*. On the antique tables and wooden bookcases. On an old trunk. On the fireplace mantel. Even on the floor. The whole room smelled of hot wax.

Creepy!

My eyes darted to the windows. They were draped with curtains. Heavy black curtains that blocked out all the light. No wonder the house had seemed deserted from outside.

"Let's get out of here!" Liv whispered.

"Okay. Okay. As soon as he gives us our candy." I stared around the room some more. I'd never seen anything like it.

Crystals were grouped around every candle. Pink and purple crystals, glowing in the candlelight.

But the creepiest thing of all were the clocks. Clocks on the tables. Clocks on the bookcases. Clocks on the walls.

All ticking. Ticking. Ticking.

So many clocks.

The boy with the claw just stood there in the middle of the room, staring at us. I wondered if maybe he forgot about our candy.

"Do you, um, go to Shadyside Middle School?" Liv tried to make conversation with him.

"No. I go to a private school," he answered in a raspy voice. "My name is Ricky. I have a sore throat."

I studied Ricky's face. His skin was pale—so pale I could see the blue veins underneath.

"What are your names?" he croaked.

"I'm Liv." Liv shot me a let's-go-now look from the corner of her eye.

"My name is Greg—and I'm kind of in a hurry," I told Ricky. "See, I'm trying to get more candy than a friend of mine."

"I think I can help you," a sharp voice behind me replied.

23

I spun around and stared into the speckled gray eyes of an old woman.

She wore a black velvet shirt and a long skirt. Gold bracelets jangled from her bony wrists.

She was short and thin—as thin as Ricky. Her gray hair hung in wisps around her face. Her skin was lined with deep, deep wrinkles.

Everything about her seemed old—except her voice. Her voice was strong and clear.

The old woman walked up to me. She moved briskly. Not like an old woman at all.

She snatched my trick-or-treat bag from my grasp.

"Hey! Where are you going with that?" I asked, surprised. But she left the room without a word.

Ricky sat down on a shredded couch. He sat and stared at us. Just stared.

The place was really giving me the creeps.

"Greg, I want to go—" Liv began. Then she broke off and gasped. "Look!"

I followed her gaze to a shadowy corner of the room—where two large, glowing eyes peered at us.

I took a sharp breath.

I stared into those glowing yellow eyes.

Then I realized. "It's just an owl," I said, relieved. "An owl sitting on top of a grandfather clock."

"I thought owls were supposed to be smart. This one must be pretty stupid to hang around here," Liz muttered.

I laughed. "It's dumber than you think, Liv. It's stuffed."

"I want to go *now!*" Liv was twisting her bandage around her fingers like crazy.

I wanted to go too, to be honest. Not only did this house give me the creeps, I was also starting to sweat inside my werewolf costume. "Okay. If the old lady doesn't come back in a minute, we'll—"

"Shhh," Liv interrupted me. "Do you hear that?"

I listened.

I heard chanting.

Low chanting. Coming from another room.

I listened closely. It was the weird old woman's voice. But I couldn't make out the words. She was speaking in some foreign language. A language I'd never even heard before.

"What is she doing?" I asked Ricky.

Ricky didn't answer. He just stared at me.

He was making me nervous. Why didn't he talk? I stepped over to an antique table and picked up an old leather book that was resting there.

"Whoa," I whispered when I read the title. Silently I pointed it out to Liv.

In worn gold lettering it said: *Magic.*

"That's it. I'm out of here." Liz headed for the door. I was right on her heels.

And then, all of a sudden, the old lady stood in front of us. Between us and the door.

How did she get there?

"Going so soon?" she asked. "You can't leave without this." She handed me a big orange cloth bag with a jack-o'-lantern stitched on the front.

"Hey! This isn't my bag! This is a different bag!"

I glanced inside. My candy! I'd swear some of it was missing. The pile definitely looked smaller than before.

What did this weird old lady do with my bag? And my candy?

I handed the bag back to the old woman. "I want *my* bag!"

"Take this one." The old woman shoved the bag into my hand. "Take it—and don't worry about it. You'll have more candy than your friend. Then you'll come back and thank me—won't you?"

A small smile spread across her lips—and every clock in the house began to gong.

The room thundered with the sound of the clocks—gonging, chiming, ringing, bonging.

Liv covered her ears and ran to the door.

I took the bag.

But I was never coming back, I could tell you that.

The old woman opened the door. We ran out and sprinted down the steps. Liv raced down Fear Street.

"Wait up!" I yelled. "We can't go home yet. That old lady stole my candy! We have to collect more! Otherwise I won't win!"

26

"It's too late," Liv shouted. "It's ten o'clock. It's too late for trick-or-treating."

Liv was right. It was too late.

I glanced down and spotted a Tootsie Roll on the ground. I tossed it into my bag.

Whoa. Big deal. A whole night of trick-or-treating—and my bag wasn't even half filled.

Liv and I walked slowly to my house. There was Derek, pacing back and forth on my porch. "Okay, Dreamer," he called as I plodded up the front steps. "It's time to crown the trick-or-treat champ!"

"Yeah, yeah," I mumbled.

Give up, I told myself as we headed inside. *Face it— you're just not lucky.*

Up in my bedroom, Derek lifted his bag high over my bed.

He tilted it slowly—and a mountain of candy spilled out.

"Your turn!" He grinned.

I gripped the bottom of my bag.

I turned it over.

I spilled it out—and gasped in shock.

5

Candy!

Tons of candy.

Streaming out of my bag. Showering down on my bed.

Snickers bars. Candy corn. Milky Ways. M&M's. Bubble gum. Lollipops. Tootsie Rolls. Reese's Pieces.

At least ten of each kind!

Tons and tons of candy!

Much more than Derek!

"You said your bag was practically empty!" Liv stared in amazement at the mountain of treats on the bed.

"It—It was," I stammered.

"I *lost?*" Derek said in disbelief. He glared at me.

A grin spread across my face. *Yes!*

"I won! I did it! I won!" I pumped my fist in the air. "I told you I'd beat you!" I whacked Derek on the back.

Derek crumpled his trick-or-treat bag into a tight ball. He threw it on the floor. He stormed out of my room. We heard his footsteps pound down the stairs.

"I won! I won! I won!" I cheered. "I finally won!"

"I don't have anywhere near this much! Greg—how *did* you get so much candy?" Liv sifted her hands through the huge pile.

I stared down at it. "I don't know," I admitted.

Princess darted into my room just then and leaped into my pile of candy. Raina ran into my room, chasing after her.

"Wow!" Raina eyed my bed. She plunged her hands down to the bottom of the pile. Then she brought them up fast, flinging candy everywhere.

I scowled at her. "Get out of my room, Raina!"

"Make me." Raina sat down. She grabbed a candy bar, ripped off the wrapper, and took a big bite.

"Who said you could have that?" I snatched the candy bar from her.

"I don't want your stupid candy anyway." Raina jumped up and marched out of my room. "It stinks."

Liv stared at the pile of Halloween loot, shaking her head.

"I just don't get it." She took the trick-or-treat bag

from me and stared inside. "Where did all that candy come from?"

She turned the bag over and over in her hands. She examined it from every angle.

I watched her. At last I cleared my throat.

"Are you thinking what I'm thinking?" I asked.

Slowly, Liv nodded.

"The bag must be magic," she declared. "There's no other explanation."

I took a deep breath. I picked up a Snickers bar and tossed it into the trick-or-treat bag.

I held the bag closed for a few seconds.

Then I opened it and peeked inside.

"Wow!" I cried. "Ten! There are *ten* Snickers bars in here!" I spilled them out for Liv to see.

Liv's eyes practically popped out of her head.

We both stared at the bag in silence.

It was unbelievable.

Liv handed the bag back to me. She unwrapped one of the candy bars and took a bite. Then she wrinkled her nose. "You know, Raina's right."

"Huh? About what?"

"This candy stinks. It tastes funny."

I took a bite from her candy bar. "No it doesn't. It tastes fine to me."

I sat down on my bed. I studied the bag. "That old lady must have put some kind of spell on it. This is so cool! Let's try something else!"

I lifted my glass baseball trophy off my desk.

No. I changed my mind. I wasn't sure what the bag would do, and I didn't want anything to happen to my trophy.

I grabbed my baseball instead.

I tossed it into the bag.

I closed the bag. I waited a few seconds, then turned it over.

Ten baseballs came rolling out!

Then I threw in my limited-edition Superman comic.

Ten comics came out. *Ten!*

"I have ten limited-edition Superman comics!" I shouted.

"Greg!" Liv gasped. "You're going to be rich!"

"I know! These are worth a fortune!" I fanned the valuable comics in my hand.

"That's not what I mean!" Liv's eyes lit with excitement. She dug into her pocket and came up with a ten-dollar bill.

"Put it in the bag!" she said. "Let's see if it works!"

6

I placed the ten-dollar bill in the bag. I closed the bag.

Then I closed my eyes and prayed. *Please work! Please work!*

"Give me that!" Liv grabbed the bag and peered inside.

"Well? Did it work?" I demanded. "Did it?"

"Yes!" Liv shrieked. "It worked! It worked!"

She turned the bag upside down. *Ten* ten-dollar bills showered down on us.

One hundred dollars!

"I'm rich! I'm rich!" I cried.

Liv picked up the money from the floor. She stared at it. "No—no, you're not rich," she said.

"Wh-what do you mean?" I stammered.

"I'm rich!" she shouted. "That was my money! I'm rich!"

"Ha-ha. You're a riot." I reached into the top drawer of my night table and pulled out a twenty-dollar bill. I was saving it for new drumsticks. But this was an emergency.

I put it in the bag. Closed the bag. Turned it upside down.

Two hundred dollars came out!

Liv and I stared at our money.

"We have *three hundred dollars!"* she gasped.

"It's amazing!" I cried. "Wait until I tell Mom and Dad about this bag. Hey, Mom!" I started toward my door.

"Wait!" Liv jumped up and clapped her hand over my mouth. "You can't do that!" she declared. "They'll take the bag away from you. They'll make you turn it in to the police or something!"

Whoa. I never thought of that. Good thing Liv was around!

I pried her hand away from my mouth. "You're right," I agreed. "We better keep it a secret."

"Great." Liv stacked our money into a neat pile. "Let's go to the Division Street Mall tomorrow. Let's go shopping!"

Saturday morning I got up early.

I couldn't wait to go to the mall!

I got dressed really fast.

Raina popped into my room as I was tying my sneakers. "Where are you going?"

"To the mall with Liv," I told her.

"I want to go too," Raina said.

"No way!"

"If you don't take me, I'll rip up all your comic books when you're gone." Raina grabbed my ten limited-edition comics from my desk.

"Give those back!" I yanked them from her and tossed them behind me on the bed.

Raina pointed to the bed and laughed.

Princess sat there, batting the pages with her paw.

I rolled my eyes. "Take Princess and go," I ordered, handing the cat to Raina. "And I'm warning you — stay out of my room!"

Raina left and I finished getting dressed. I hid my comics under some clothes on the top shelf of my closet—just in case.

Then I raced over to Liv's. We hurried to the Division Street Mall.

"I want to go to Music World first," Liv said as we walked into the mall.

So that's where we headed. And wouldn't you know it? The first person we bumped into was Derek.

"Hey, Derek! I bet I can buy more CDs than you!" I declared.

"Forget about betting, Greg!" Liv said. "You already won last night. Don't start acting stupid again." She sounded irritated.

"It's too late." Derek laughed. "Greg is already stupid—he forgot that I always have more money than he does. Always!"

He reached into his wallet and took out two twenties and a ten. Fifty dollars. He fanned it in front of my face. "Beat that, Dreamer."

I reached into my windbreaker pocket and waved my money in front of him—my two hundred dollars.

Derek turned pale.

"This isn't over!" he shouted.

Then he stomped out of the store.

"What a sore loser!" I laughed.

"Come on already." Liv tugged me over to the CD rack.

We picked out fifteen CDs. The store was crowded, so it took a while to pay for them. But I didn't care. I was rich! Nothing could spoil my mood.

"Where do you want to go next?" Liv asked as we reached the door.

"How about—" I began.

A wailing alarm pierced the air.

A tall, beefy security guard stepped in front of us. Right in front of the door.

"You two!" he barked, glaring at us. "Stop right there!"

7

The guard grabbed our arms and pulled us toward the back of the store. His fingers were clamped firmly around my bicep.

"What's going on? Wh-Where are we going?" I stammered.

"To the police," he said gruffly.

"The police!" Liv gasped. "Why? We didn't do anything wrong!"

"That's what they all say," the guard grumbled.

"What did we do?" Liv wailed. "Are you going to send us to jail?"

The guard didn't answer.

He marched us through the aisles.

Oh no! We are going to jail, I thought. *We're going to jail—and I don't even know why!*

As we stumbled through the crowded store, the other shoppers gawked at us. They shook their heads and frowned. They shrank back from us.

"Here they are." The guard delivered us to a short, chubby man with round cheeks and a black mustache. His Music World name tag read MANAGER.

A few wisps of black hair fell over his forehead. Except for those wisps, he was bald. A pair of reading glasses perched on the tip of his nose. He peered over their tops, shifting his gaze from me to Liv.

"Where did you get this?" he asked, holding up a handful of tens and twenties. I guessed they must be the bills we used to pay for the CDs.

I shot a glance at Liv.

Her face was pale. She twisted her braid around her fingers.

"Well?" the manager demanded.

"We, um, found it," I murmured.

The manager studied my face for a moment. Then he studied the bills in his hand. "They're counterfeit," he finally said. "They're not real."

"No way! That can't be!" I exclaimed.

"They're not real," he repeated. "Feel this." He held out one of my twenty-dollar bills. I rubbed my fingers over it.

Then he reached into his pocket and took out another twenty-dollar bill. "Now touch this one," he ordered.

I touched it.

"It feels different!" I gasped. My fingers started to tremble.

The manager fanned my money in his palm. "Bad counterfeits," he said. "More like play money."

My heart pounded in my chest.

Oh no! We are going to jail!

The manager took a step back from us. "You look like nice kids. I've seen you in the store before. Now tell me the truth. Did you really *find* this money?" He narrowed his eyes at me.

"Yes. We really did," I answered. "Honest."

Well, it was as close to the truth as I was going to get. No way was I going to try to explain about the magic bag!

"Okay. Give me back the CDs," the manager told me.

My hands shook as I gave him the bag.

"I'm going to let you go—this time. But there had better not be a next time," he said sternly.

I gulped. "Yes sir. I mean, no sir. I mean—"

"Come on," Liv broke in.

We left the store as quickly as we could. Liv was shaking so much, we headed for a bench so she could sit down.

"I don't believe that!" Her voice quivered.

Then she jumped up from the bench.

"This is all your fault!" she shouted.

"My fault?" I glared at her. "You were the one who wanted to put money in the bag in the first place! How is it my fault?"

"Because I *told* you something was wrong with that candy! I *told* you it didn't taste right! And now something is wrong with the money too."

Liv pulled out her fake money and tore it up.

"Well, that's not my fault," I declared. "It's the bag's fault! How was I supposed to know it didn't make perfect copies? How was I supposed to know the copies were a little, well, off?"

"I told you," Liv insisted.

We argued about whose fault it was all the way to my house.

We argued about it all the way up to my room.

We were still arguing about it as we walked through my bedroom doorway.

And then we stopped arguing about it—when we saw Raina in my room. Sitting on my bed.

With the trick-or-treat bag in her lap.

She was reaching inside it. With something in her hand.

"Don't, Raina!" I screamed. "Don't put *that* in the bag!"

8

Raina plunged her hand deeper into the bag.

"No! *Stop!*" I leaped across the room. "Don't put the hamster in there!"

I grabbed Raina's wrist. I jerked it out of the bag, hard.

Her hand came out—with the hamster sitting in her palm.

"That was a close one." I let out a sigh.

"Ow! You're hurting me! Let go." Raina wrenched free of my grip.

I snatched the bag away from her. "I told you to stay out of here!" I yelled, tossing the bag across the room.

"Greg! Look!" Liv screamed. She stared across the room in horror.

I followed her gaze—and screamed too.

Princess was crawling inside the bag.

"Princess, *no!* Get out of there!" I dove for the bag. Too late.

She was completely inside it.

I tried to grab the bag, but I couldn't.

It leaped around on the floor. It jerked wildly from side to side. Snarls and hisses filled the air.

"Wow!" Raina stared wide-eyed. "It looks like Princess is fighting another cat in there!"

I really hoped she was wrong.

Finally I pounced on the bag. I lay on top of it. It jerked and twitched for a second. Then it stopped.

My heart pounded as I sat up and let go.

Princess scrambled out.

Followed by another Princess.

And another Princess. And another. And another. And another.

"Oh *noooo!*" I moaned.

I watched in horror as ten white cats filled my room. One jumped on my desk and pawed at my glass baseball trophy.

It started to topple.

"Greg!" Liv screamed. "Get it!"

I leaped across the room—and caught the trophy

before it fell. "Whew! That was close!" I said, holding it up.

"Not that!" she hollered. "The bag!"

I whirled around—and saw two cats crawl back into the bag. The bag jerked and hopped across the room. It was totally out of control!

The second I wrestled it to the ground, twenty more cats scrambled out!

"Oh nooooo," I moaned.

Now I had almost *thirty* cats in my small room.

Cats creeping on my desk, stretching on my bed, tiptoeing along on my bookshelves, padding across my drum set.

Every inch of carpet was covered with cats. So many they couldn't walk without bumping into each other.

They swarmed around my ankles, meowing.

I tried to move away, but I couldn't. There was no place to go without stepping on a cat.

"Wow!" Raina's eyes opened wide in amazement. "You're in trouble now, Greg!"

"Get them!" I yelled.

Liv and I ran around the room, trying to gather up the cats. I scooped one up—and it let out a long, menacing hiss.

"Ow!" Liv screamed as another cat sank its teeth into her ankle.

I picked up a third cat.

I cuddled it in my arms. "Nice kitty," I murmured. "Nice Princess."

The cat gave a long, throaty purr—then swiped its claws across my cheek.

"Ow!" I dropped the cat and ran my hand over my cheek.

Blood! There was blood trickling from my raw skin!

"Watch out, Greg! Behind you!" Liv yelled.

I whirled around—just in time to dodge a cat leaping from the dresser. It was aiming for my head, but it landed on my leg. Clung to it. Sank its sharp claws into my shin.

Another cat flew at me. It landed on my chest. I jerked my head back as it tried to scratch my eyes out.

"These cats aren't like Princess," Raina whimpered. She shrank back as two hissing cats moved in on her. "These cats are mean. I'm going back to my room." Cradling her hamster in her hands, she darted out.

The terrifying cats tore at my bedspread. My curtains. My carpet. They batted my books off the shelves. They ripped my homework to shreds. They chewed through my pillow.

"There's something wrong with these cats!" I cried. "They're vicious! It's the bag's fault! They're *not* like Princess! The bag changed them!"

Liv backed herself against a wall. "This isn't working," she shouted. "We can't pick up these cats!"

I shielded my face with my hands as another cat hurled itself at me.

"What else can we do?" I wailed. "We have to get rid of them. We can't just leave them here! Do you have a better idea?"

Liv peeled a cat off her leg and gazed at me with narrowed eyes. "Yes, I do," she said. "I have an idea—but you're not going to like it."

9

"**M**uffin? Use Muffin to get rid of the cats! No way!"
I declared.

We were standing in the hall outside my room.
Inside, nearly thirty cats yowled and scratched at the
door. Liv had grabbed the bag while I cleared a path
to the door.

"It's the *only* way," Liv insisted. "The way to get
rid of cats is with dogs. The dogs will chase the cats
out! If you have a better idea, let's hear it!"

I didn't have a better idea—so we sneaked out of
my house and over to Mrs. O'Connor's yard.

Muffin was lying on the walkway. The second he
caught sight of us he let out a growl. His lip curled
back to bare his teeth.

"I don't like this," I muttered, staring at the crazy dog. Muffin was little, but he was mean.

"We have no choice," Liv reminded me. "Do you remember the plan?"

I nodded. The plan. That's what had me worried.

Liv marched up to Muffin.

He trained his eyes on her. Watching her. Waiting to see what she was up to.

I tiptoed up behind him—and threw the trick-or-treat bag over him.

"Arf! Grff! Rowf!" Inside the bag, Muffin erupted in furious barks and snarls.

"Got him!" I cried. "Let's go!"

Liv helped me scoop the bag up.

I held it closed, but it wasn't easy. Muffin struggled like a maniac.

We started back to my house. Liv held up the bottom of the bag. I clutched the top. Muffin barked madly.

"Hurry! Run. Before Mrs. O'Connor hears him!" Liv grunted.

Mom and Dad were in the living room, near the front door, so we had to sneak in through the back.

"What's all that noise?" Mom called to us as we struggled up the steps with the bag.

"Just a new CD Liv's playing on her boom box," I answered, gasping for breath. "Sorry. We'll lower the volume."

46

We reached my bedroom. I threw open the door.

We dropped the bag on the floor—and ten furious Muffins burst out of the bag.

Luckily for us, the dogs forgot all about us the moment they spotted the cats. The dogs eyed their prey in menacing silence.

The cats returned their gaze. Their fur bristled. They arched their backs.

I hope this works, I prayed. *It's got to work. It's just got to!*

The dogs curled back their lips.

They bared their fangs.

They opened their jaws—

And *quacked!*

10

Quack. Quack. Quack.

The dogs waddled around the room, quacking like ducks.

"Oh no!" I wailed.

"This is horrible!" Liv groaned.

The bag! It messed up—again! It made duck-dogs!

The cats snarled and spat at the quacking terriers.

My room seethed with animals. Hissing cats wove between my feet. Quacking dogs surged around my ankles. There were so many of them, I couldn't even see my rug anymore.

I started to feel dizzy. So many animals in such a small space!

Then . . . the cats leaped at the dogs. With claws

bared, they tore after them. Quacking and yelping, the dogs ran for cover.

The room echoed with hissing, screeching, and quacking.

"It didn't work! Your stupid idea didn't work!" I yelled at Liv. "The dogs were supposed to chase the cats! But instead the cats are chasing the dogs!"

"It's not my fault. It's the bag's fault!" Liv snapped.

We watched as the cats pounced on the dogs.

Quack! Quack! Quack! The dogs tried frantically to escape. But I guess they weren't cut out for waddling.

Some just toppled over. Others tried to hide in my closet. Still others tried to squeeze under the bed.

One dog scrambled up on my drum set. He lost his balance and sent my drums and cymbals toppling over. They landed on the floor with a deafening *crash!*

"Greg!" Mom called up the stairs.

Uh-oh.

Now I was in real trouble.

I picked my way back to the door and opened it a crack. "What, Mom?" I called, trying to sound innocent.

"What is all that noise?" she demanded.

"Greg! Look out!" Liv shouted.

The dogs had followed me to the door.

They waddled out of the room.

The cats ran after them, chasing them down the steps.

My legs were all tangled up in cats and dogs. I couldn't stop them. I couldn't stop *myself*. It was all I could do to keep my balance as they dragged me downstairs with them. "Watch out, Mom!" I yelled.

My mother leaped back as I lunged for the front door. I opened it—and the cats chased the dogs right out of the house.

"Greg! *What* are you doing?" Mom gaped at the fleeing animals in shock.

I gulped. "Uh . . . Just cleaning my room."

Liv and I dashed out of the house before Mom or Dad could say another word. We ran past Mrs. O'Connor's house.

"Muffin . . . Where are you?" I heard her calling. "Muffin! Time to eat!"

We kept running.

We didn't stop until we reached the park on the other side of town.

Out of breath, we collapsed on the grass under a tree.

I closed my eyes—and pictured my room filled with hissing cats and quacking dogs.

"That was really scary!" I admitted to Liv.

I leaned back against the tree and sighed. Then I bolted upright as I thought of something terrible.

"Oh no!" I cried. "Princess! The real Princess! She must have run out with all the other cats. I wonder where she is?"

"Don't worry. I'm sure she'll find her way back home," Liv said. "But we *do* have to worry about that stupid trick-or-treat bag! We have to get rid of it, Greg. It's way too dangerous to have hanging around."

"I know. But I'm glad I had it," I said. I relaxed against the tree again. "It helped me beat Derek."

"The competition isn't over, Dreamer," Derek's voice said.

I jumped to my feet as he stepped out from behind the tree.

"How long were you there?" I demanded. "Were you spying on us?"

"Spying on you? Oh, please." Derek shook his head. "I've got better things to do, Dreamer."

"Like what?" I sneered.

A smug smile crept across Derek's face. "Like hanging out in my uncle's brand-new candy store." His smile grew broader. "Now I have so much more candy than you, it isn't even funny!"

I could feel my face begin to turn red.

How is this possible? I asked myself.

How can Derek have such good luck? How?

"And guess what else?" he went on. "Look what my grandmother gave me."

He shoved a thick stack of money in my face. "Five hundred dollars for my birthday today! Now I have more money than you, too," he bragged.

Derek's birthday is today? I thought miserably. How can I have such *bad* luck!

"I beat you!" Derek crowed. "I beat you after all!"

"No you didn't!" I blurted out. "I can have one thousand dollars by tomorrow!"

"Greg!" Liv warned.

I ignored her. "Just come to my house—and you'll see," I told Derek.

"Yeah, right." Derek smirked.

"Afraid you'll lose the bet?" I taunted.

"Ha. No chance. I'll see you tomorrow, loser." Derek walked off, laughing.

"Yeah. You're the loser, loser," I muttered to his back.

I strode out of the park. I was going home—home for the trick-or-treat bag.

"Greg, wait!" Liv ran after me. "I know what you're up to. You can't use that bag again! It's too dangerous!"

"I have to use it!" I told her. "Just one more time. I have to beat Derek!"

"But the money it makes is no good! It's counterfeit!"

"It looked real enough to fool us," I reminded her. "It will fool Derek, too. That's all I need."

52

I ran the rest of the way home. I couldn't wait to start making money—way more money than Derek. Liv ran next to me, trying to talk me out of it. But she was wasting her breath.

I ran up to my room.

The bag wasn't on the floor where I had left it.

In fact, I didn't see it anywhere.

"Where is it?" I muttered.

My heart began to pound. My eyes darted frantically around the room. Where was that bag? I needed it to beat Derek!

"Calm down. It has to be here somewhere," Liv assured me.

"It has to be—because I need it!" I cried. "I need a thousand dollars by tomorrow!"

I spun in a circle, searching everywhere.

But the bag was gone.

11

"Where is it?" I cried. "Where is my trick-or-treat bag?"

My books were back on the shelves. My homework sat neatly on my desk. The bed was made.

But there was no sign of the bag.

I threw my shoes out from under the bed, searching for it.

I flung the clothes out of my drawers.

I scattered the papers on my desk.

I couldn't find it anywhere.

"Stop looking!" Liv pleaded. "Forget about the bag!"

"But I need it!" I insisted. "If only I can find it, I can beat Derek once and for all."

I tore open the closet door. Started pulling clothes off the hangers. "Where is it? Where is it?"

"Greg!" Mom yelled. *"What* are you doing in here?"

I glanced up. She stood in the doorway with her arms crossed over her chest. "I just cleaned up your room. Now look at what you've done!"

"But Mom—"

"And you left it a mess after I told you to clean it up! Bringing all those animals in here. I tell you, Greg, I'm starting to lose patience with you."

"But Mom, I—"

"And my reading group is going to be here any minute. So clean this place—right now!" Mom turned to leave.

"Mom, *wait!*" I yelled.

She stopped in the doorway and raised her eyebrows at me.

I took a deep breath. "Did you see a big trick-or-treat bag with orange handles and a jack-o'-lantern on the front?"

"Yes. I did."

"Great! What did you do with it?"

"I tossed all your trash into it," she said.

Liv and I glanced nervously at each other.

"You put stuff *in* the bag?" I asked.

"Yes. That's what I said—I tossed all your trash into it. Then I threw the bag out."

I let out a gasp. "You threw the bag out?"

The doorbell rang.

"That must be my reading group." Mom hurried down the stairs to greet them.

"Oh no, Liv! She threw the bag out!" I bolted across the room to check my wastepaper basket.

Empty.

Liv and I tore through the second floor. We searched all the wastepaper baskets.

All empty.

"Face it, Greg," Liv said. "That bag is history."

"No, it's not." I snapped my fingers. "I know! Today is garbage day. It's probably in the garbage can out front!"

Liv and I raced downstairs. Mom's reading group was getting settled in the living room, so we had to run to the back door.

We dashed around to the front of the house.

Our big green garbage can sat by the curb.

I lifted the lid—and let out a long moan.

The garbage can was empty! The garbage truck had already come!

"Now what am I going to do?" I sat down on the curb with my head in my hands. "I need that bag."

"I still say you're better off without it," Liv declared. "I'm glad it's gone."

Gone.

My magic trick-or-treat bag was gone. Taken away by the trash collectors.

I bet Derek that I would have a thousand dollars. I bet him that I'd have it by tomorrow—and he was coming to see it.

I pictured his face when I showed him nothing.

He's never going to let me live this down, I realized.

"I can't lose this bet with Derek," I moaned. "I just can't."

Liv shrugged her shoulders.

"How much money do you have?" I asked her.

"None."

I checked my jeans pockets.

Empty.

I'm a loser, I thought. A big loser. What am I going to do now? Should I just leave town?

And then I heard it. The rumble of the garbage truck. It was grinding around the corner, heading back to the dump.

With my trick-or-treat bag in it. Somewhere.

"Come on, Liv!" I jumped up from the curb. "We have to catch that truck!"

12

I raced after the garbage truck.

The traffic light turned red on the corner of the next block. The garbage truck rumbled to a stop.

Yes! I thought.

I can catch it now!

I picked up speed.

I ran so hard I thought my lungs would burst.

The truck stood half a block away. The light remained red.

"Wait! I need my garbage back!" I shouted to the man behind the wheel.

The light turned green.

The truck didn't move.

He heard me!

I ran faster. My sneakers pounded the ground. I was almost there. I could almost touch the truck.

And then it pulled away.

"Oh no," I groaned. "He didn't hear me."

I started to run again. But the driver stepped hard on the gas. In seconds, the truck was disappearing down the road, blocks and blocks away, a tiny speck now.

Out of breath and disappointed, I trudged back to my house. Liv was still standing out front. She hadn't moved.

"Sorry. But it's the best thing that could have happened," she said as I walked up. "That bag was too weird."

I guess she was trying to make me feel better.

But she made me feel worse.

"Of course the bag was weird—it was a *magic* bag!" I shouted. "And you can't just give up a magic bag! We have to get it back. We have to go to the dump and find it."

"Are you nuts?" Liv yelled. "There's tons of garbage at the dump. We'll never find the stupid bag."

"If we hurry we will," I insisted. "It will be easy."

"We are not going to find that bag," Liv argued.

"Why not?"

"Because *we* are not going." Liv started to walk away. *"You* are going—without me. Good luck."

Good luck—I knew I couldn't count on that.

I needed Liv's help.

"Wait!" I called after her. "What if I promise to use the bag just one more time. Just once—so I can make the thousand dollars to beat Derek. Then I promise I'll get rid of it. Will you help me find it?"

Liv sat down on the curb, thinking. She twisted her braid around her finger.

I didn't want to rush her.

But we needed to get to the dump fast, before the bag was completely buried in trash.

I couldn't wait any longer. "Come on, Liv," I urged. "We have to hurry. Or we'll lose it forever!"

"Okay, okay," she finally agreed.

The dump was way out at the western edge of Shadyside. We ran the whole way there.

I'd never actually visited the place. But I knew it was on Oak Street. And I could tell from the smell when we got close.

Phew! What a stink.

We followed our noses, turned a corner—and there it was. Behind a tall wire fence—mountains and mountains of garbage. Some were piled way higher than my house.

"I'm not going in there! Look!" Liv shrieked. "Vultures!"

Clouds of dark birds circled the heaps. They dove down. Then snapped up bits of rancid food from the stinking mounds.

"Liv. They're not vultures. They're pigeons," I told her as I pulled her through a hole in the fence.

We walked around the tall piles of trash.

They smelled worse than rotten eggs. Worse than sour milk. Worse than skunk. Worse than all those three put together.

I almost gagged on the horrible stench. But I held my nose and pressed on. I had to find that bag!

"Ewwww!" Liv shrieked. "Get this off of me! Get it off now!" She jumped up and down like a maniac.

I turned to see her cheek smeared with brown glop.

I didn't know what the gooey stuff was, but it smelled really awful—and there were flies stuck in it.

I didn't want to make a big deal of it, so I wiped it off with my jacket sleeve. Yuck.

Then we continued to search.

I sifted through some small piles of trash.

I poked at some rotting cardboard boxes.

Nothing.

I turned in a circle and gazed at the mounds and mounds of garbage. It would take forever to search through it all.

"Hey! What's that?" Liv pointed to a small hill of trash a few feet ahead of us.

From the top, two orange handles peeked up—just like the handles on my trick-or-treat bag.

Yes!

I sprinted over to the hill for a closer look.

Definitely yes!

"You're a genius! You found it!" I cheered Liv.

I started to climb up the garbage hill. My foot sank in—up to my ankle. I could feel my sneaker and sock turn wet. Wet and slimy.

I didn't stop to think about it—or to look. I had to keep going.

I climbed and climbed until I reached the bag.

"I've got it!" I grabbed the bag, waved it in the air for Liv to see—and lost my balance.

I toppled down the other side of the garbage hill.

I rolled head over heels all the way to the bottom. I landed in a deep pit of blackish brown slime.

"Greg! Are you okay?" Liv ran around the mountain of garbage to help. "Ewww! That's disgusting." She backed away from me fast.

I was covered in the oily ooze. My clothes. My face. My hair. Drops of it clung to my eyelashes.

I tried to stand up.

My sneakers slid on the oily muck. My feet flew out from under me. I landed on my back with a sickening plop—drenched in the sludge.

"I can't get up. You'll have to help me." I reached out my hand for Liv to grab.

"You're filthy and you stink! I'm not touching you."

"Liv!"

"Okay, okay." She took my filthy hand. "Oh,

gross." Gagging and coughing, she pulled me out of the pit.

On the way back to my house, Liv walked on the other side of the street. As far away from me as she could. She couldn't stand the way I smelled.

I guess I really reeked.

We sneaked in through the back door so that Mom and her reading group wouldn't see me. I prayed they wouldn't smell me either.

I dropped the bag on my bedroom floor. Then I headed into the bathroom to wash up and change my clothes.

"Greg! Come quick! Come back here!" Liv cried.

I ran out of the bathroom—and stopped in my doorway.

Liv was standing on my bed.

"Th-the bag," she stammered, pointing to the floor. "There's something in it!"

13

The bag bulged. It twisted and curled on the floor. Then it uncurled and thrashed.

I watched in horror as it seemed to inflate—growing fuller and fuller.

"Wh-what do you think is in there?" Liv twisted her braid around her entire hand.

"I don't know." My voice was hushed and fearful. "But whatever it is, it's multiplying."

I couldn't imagine *what* was in there. The bag felt empty when I carried it home.

I watched its seams strain to keep closed.

What was in there?

Liv gasped as the bag started to pitch and reel across my room. It seemed alive now.

"Did you see my hamster?" Raina popped her head into my room. "I let him out of his cage this morning. I've looked everywhere. I can't find him."

"Oh no," I groaned. "Liv, did the hamster run in here while I was in the bathroom?"

"I—I didn't see him. But I guess he could have," she replied.

"Why are you standing on the bed?" Raina asked Liv. "Mom doesn't allow that."

"It's your fault!" I told my sister as I reached for the bag. "If you hadn't let your hamster out—"

I carefully lifted up one of the handles of the bag. I peeked inside—and cried out in shock.

"Cockroaches!"

Thousands of cockroaches swarmed out of the bag.

They surged into my room.

They moved across the floor in waves. A brown sea of disgusting cockroaches.

With wriggling antennae, they probed the air— then scattered!

They scampered up the curtains and along my furniture. They swarmed over my desk.

Streams of them continued to pour out of the bag. They must have made a nest in there—and then multiplied!

Within seconds, the floor, the walls, and the ceiling were alive with scurrying roaches.

Raina opened her mouth to scream, but no sound came out. She ran from the room.

The roaches crawled up my bed, along my blanket—and up Liv's legs.

"Get them off me!" She jumped up and down on the mattress, shrieking.

Roaches crawled up my pants. They crawled up my arms. I swiped them away. Swiped madly.

But they kept coming.

And then they started to bite.

I suddenly felt hundreds of tiny nips all over my body. "Ow!" I yelled. "Ow! Ouch!"

"Yeow!" Liv screamed, slapping at her arms and legs. "They're eating me!"

"Roaches aren't supposed to bite!" I yelled.

"It's the bag's fault!" Liv screamed. "The copies it makes are evil, Greg!"

I felt a roach creep across my cheek.

I swatted it from my face.

Another one dropped from the ceiling—and landed in my hair.

"Oooooo!" I brushed my hand through my hair quickly. I hung my head down and shook it hard.

I spun around to the mirror to see if it was gone— but I couldn't see a thing.

The mirror was covered with a thick, brown blanket—a living blanket of roaches.

66

They crawled in and out of my VCR, my radio, my TV.

"What are we going to do?" Liv wailed. She batted roaches from her neck. "This is all your fault! I told you to leave that bag where it was! I told you it was dangerous!"

Her hand flew up to her face. "Oh, *gross!*" She flicked one out of her ear. "Do something!" she screamed.

I crossed the room to get my baseball mitt. I'll try to scoop them up, I thought.

I took a few steps—and let out a moan.

A carpet of roaches crunched under my feet.

I sucked in a deep breath and lunged across the room for my glove.

Then I started to scoop.

That's when the roaches started to fly.

14

The roaches didn't just *fly*.

They *dive-bombed* us.

They swooped down from the ceiling and zoomed at our faces. The room hummed with the sound of their wings.

"Greg, this is a nightmare!" Liv cried out. "They're attacking us! Roaches are *not* supposed to do that!"

A squadron of roaches soared at me. I batted them back. I swiped furiously at them.

They circled me.

They landed on my head. I could feel their legs— hundreds of roach legs—crawling over my scalp.

I scratched and scratched—and they flew into my

ears. They scuttled across my face. Their sharp legs pricked my eyelids.

I shook my head wildly, trying to get them off.

A brown cloud of the insects dove for Liv.

"Watch out!" I screamed—and a roach flew into my mouth.

It lodged in my throat.

My stomach heaved.

I started to gag.

I opened my mouth and forced myself to cough. I bent over and coughed hard. Finally the bug flew out of my mouth.

"Ooooo, gross. *Gross!*" I collapsed on the floor.

CRUNCH! CRUNCH!

Yuck!

Liv leaped off the bed. "We can't catch this many roaches. We have to get out of here. They're out of control!"

She raced into the hallway.

I got up and ran out after her—and gasped.

The hall was a moving brown river of roaches. Roaches marching toward Raina's bedroom—and Mom and Dad's too.

"We have to stop them!" I ran to the linen closet and pulled out a stack of towels.

"Quick!" I told Liv. "Close the bedroom doors and block the bottoms with these." I tossed a thick stack of towels to her.

I ran to Raina's room. It was right next to mine.

Raina sat under her blankets. "I found him," she said meekly, cuddling her hamster. They both shivered with fear.

"Just stay there," I told her. "You'll be okay." I slammed her door shut and blocked the cracks with towels.

"No roaches here," Liv called from Mom and Dad's room down the hall.

She closed the door and sealed off the bottom with some towels.

I headed across the hall to the bathroom.

Too late.

Roaches skittered across the white tile floor. They swarmed in the tub. They crept over the toilet seat.

I peered into the toilet bowl—and saw at least fifty of them paddling around.

Ugh.

I raced for the steps—and froze.

Thousands of roaches swarmed down the stairs.

They crawled along the banister.

They scuttled along the walls.

They soared through the air.

The ones crawling down the steps were the worst. I watched in horror as the big ones scurried right over the backs of the little ones in a race to get down.

70

"Roaches! Roaches!" Shrieks and cries rose suddenly from the living room.

Oh, no!

Mom's reading group!

I bolted down the steps, two at a time, trying to ignore the crunching under my feet.

I peeked into the living room.

Everyone was hopping desperately around the room. Leaping and jumping over the roaches. One lady was standing in the middle of the coffee table, screaming.

I winced as a huge roach fluttered into her mouth. I should have warned her about opening her mouth.

Everyone swatted at the bugs. Batted them. Stomped on them.

"This is disgusting!" a tall, thin woman cried. "I'm leaving."

She picked up her book—and let out a scream. A small army of roaches crawled out from between the pages. They marched up her fingers.

"Ouch! They bite!" she wailed.

I watched as all the color drained from Mom's face.

She chased after the roaches with a dish towel. "I'm so sorry," she apologized in a frantic voice. "I don't know where they came from. I really don't. I've never had this problem before."

Mom swung the dish towel around the room.

Smacking, beating, slapping, whacking at the horrible bugs.

It wasn't working.

They scattered to other parts of the room.

I glanced up the steps.

More roaches headed down.

A lot more.

"Greg! Help!" Mom spotted me, her eyes wide with panic. "Get the bug spray. *Hurry!*"

I raced into the kitchen. I searched under the sink for the spray.

We didn't have any.

It wouldn't have worked anyway. Mom didn't know it, but we had thousands and thousands of roaches. We'd need a tank of that stuff to get rid of them.

"What are you going to do?" Liv met me in the kitchen. She kept scratching at her skin. "How are you going to get rid of them?"

"We can't do this alone," I said.

I tore back upstairs.

Crunch. Crunch. Crunch.

Cockroaches crunched under my pounding feet.

I grabbed the trick-or-treat bag.

I shook it to make sure it was empty. Then I raced back downstairs. I grabbed Liv and we ran out of the house.

We charged through the neighborhood.

"Where are we going?" Liv panted.

"Don't worry! Just follow me!"

"Follow you *where?*" she asked, gulping for air.

"We need help!" I cried. "We're going for help!"

"Where?" Liv demanded.

"We have to see that old lady!" I cried. "She's the only one who can help us. We're going to Fear Street!"

15

"**F**ear Street!" Liv stopped running. "I'm not going back there. No way!"

"We have no choice, Liv. My house is crawling with cockroaches. Flying, stinging, biting cockroaches! We have to talk to that old woman. It's her bag. She knows how it works. She'll know how to get rid of them!"

I started walking.

Liv didn't move.

She planted her feet firmly on the ground. Her face turned rigid.

"You'll have to find another way to get rid of the roaches," she declared. "I'm not going with you."

"You have to go with me!" I shouted.

"Why? Why do I have to go with you? All this was your fault—not mine!" Liv yelled. "I told you not to chase after that bag. But you wouldn't listen!"

"I thought you were my best friend! But you're not! You're not even a *good* friend!" I shouted.

I didn't mean to say that to Liv. She *was* a good friend. I was just upset.

She won't take it seriously, I told myself.

She'll laugh it off—then she'll go with me.

I waited.

Liv wasn't laughing.

"Not a good friend!" she exploded. "Since this morning, I've been scratched by killer cats. I've been attacked by quacking dogs. I was nearly sent to jail. I've had garbage flies stuck to my face and cockroaches crawling in my ears. All because of *you!* I'm going home!"

"You can't go," I argued.

"Try to stop me!" Liv started to walk away.

"Please, Liv!" I chased after her. "I'm sorry about what I said. It's just that I have a big problem right now. I have to get rid of the roaches! Please, please come with me."

"No! I am not going into that creepy woman's house again!" Liv quickened her step.

"We won't go in!" I panted, trying to catch up with her. "We'll ring the bell. When the old woman comes

75

to the door, I'll ask her what to do. We'll stay on the porch. We won't go in—I promise."

Liv stopped walking.

She twisted her braid, thinking. "You really, really promise?"

I nodded.

"Okay."

"Thanks. You *are* a great friend. Now let's go!"

We raced to the old woman's house.

Fear Street was as spooky as ever. The late afternoon sun had faded, and the streetlights should have been on. But they weren't.

As we neared the end of the block, an icy wind began to blow. The tree limbs quaked and groaned in the strong gusts.

"This is it." I touched Liv's arm to stop her.

We stood directly in front of the old woman's house.

I stared at it. The grimy bricks. The totally dark windows.

"Remember—you promised we wouldn't go in." Liv's voice trembled.

I nodded.

We walked up the path to the front door.

I knocked softly at first.

No answer.

"I think this is a big mistake." Liv twisted her

braid around her fingers. "Don't knock again. We'll figure out how to get rid of the roaches ourselves. I really think we should go home."

I knocked again. A little harder this time.

The door creaked open.

Ricky, the kid we had met the first time we were there, answered. He stood in the dim light of the entranceway. Behind him I could see the glow of the candles. I could hear the clocks. Ticking. Ticking. Ticking.

"Hi, Ricky," I said. "I need to ask your, um, mother a question."

Ricky stared at us. His skin appeared even paler than before. The blue veins in his face seemed brighter.

I waited for him to say something—but he didn't.

"Um, Greg means your grandmother," Liv tried. "We have to ask your grandmother a question."

Silence.

"It will just take a second," I said.

Ricky stepped forward.

His face twisted into a scowl.

"Get away!" he said gruffly. "Get away *now!*"

16

"**G**o!" Ricky commanded. His eyes bulged open.

Liv spun around and started to leave.

"Wait!" A strong hand grasped my wrist and pulled me inside the house. "I'm so glad to see you. I knew you'd come back."

It was the old woman.

She wore the same black velvet shirt. The same long skirt. The same jewelry. Everything the same— except now she had bright orange lipstick smeared across her lips.

Her orange lips parted in an icy smile.

I did *not* want to be inside this house alone.

"Liv! Come back!" I called out the door. I could see

78

her scurrying down the path. She was nearly at the gate.

"Please come back!"

Would she really leave me here—alone with this creepy old woman?

Liv stopped.

She turned around and stared at me. She twisted her braid.

"Please!"

I let out a sigh of relief when she started back and followed me inside.

We stood close together in the big living room. It looked as creepy as it had the first time we were there.

The pink and purple crystals glowed in the candle-light.

The owl stared down at us.

The clocks ticked. Ticked loudly.

The flickering candles made our shadows shift on the walls.

Ricky shrank back, behind the old woman. His hands seemed to tremble.

"I see you brought back the bag. I knew you would. I knew you'd come back to thank me." The old woman placed a hand on my shoulder.

A chill swept through my body.

I glanced at Liv.

She stood still. Frozen. Scared.

"I, um, have a question to ask you. See, I have these roaches in my house—" I started.

"Come in. Sit down." The old woman put her other hand on Liv's shoulder. Then she shoved us toward the crumbling couch.

"My mother will be here soon to pick us up," Liv lied. "We can't stay long—"

"Yes. I'm sure your mother will be here soon," the old lady said. I could tell she didn't believe Liv. "But we have plenty of time. Now sit!"

We sat.

The woman reached out and snatched the bag from me. "Thanks for returning this. I hope you enjoyed it. Now I think I'll show you some other tricks you can do with it."

"What do you mean?" I asked.

"Watch." The old woman turned and beckoned to Ricky. "Come here!" she said sharply.

Ricky stood across from us in an unlit corner of the room. Even in the dark, I could see him shaking.

We shouldn't have come here, I thought. *Liv was right.* We should have figured out a way to get rid of the roaches ourselves.

"It-it's okay," I said. "We can come back another time to see tricks. We . . . uh . . . we really have to be going now."

I stood up to leave.

"You're not going anywhere." The old lady's voice turned rough. Her face hardened. She pushed me back down on the couch.

Liv and I stared at each other.

"Not until I show you some magic," the old woman added. Her voice softened, but that made it even creepier.

"I know a lot of tricks," she told us, smiling. "And a lot of spells. I could put a spell on you right now . . . in a blink! And you wouldn't even know it happened!"

I glanced at the table beside the couch, at the book I had seen before—the one that said *"Magic"* in gold letters.

Liv leaned over. "She's crazy," she whispered. "We've got to get out of here."

The old woman glared at us. "Don't you know it's rude to whisper?" she snarled.

I gulped. "Maybe we'll stay for one trick," I said lamely.

"Ricky! Didn't I tell you to come here?" the old woman scolded.

Ricky moved out from the corner, slowly.

"Hurry up!" She narrowed her eyes at the frail boy. "These nice children want to see some magic!"

Ricky's legs trembled as he reached the old woman.

He stood in front of her, shaking all over now.

The old woman smiled. "Are you ready, Ricky?"

She didn't wait for his answer.

She lifted the trick-or-treat bag—and yanked it down over his head!

"No! Don't!" I screamed as the old lady lowered the bag over Ricky's shoulders.

"Run, Ricky!" Liv screamed.

But Ricky stood still. Frozen.

The old woman's lips moved. Low, growling sounds came out of her lips. Words in some weird, foreign language.

I gasped.

She was casting a spell!

An icy breeze sighed through the room. The candles flickered and sputtered.

Then the old lady whipped the bag off the boy — and he was gone.

"Where is he?" I stared at the empty space where Ricky had stood. "Where did Ricky go?"

The woman gazed into my eyes. Her pupils grew large and dark. I could see the candlelight flickering in them.

"Why, he's right here." She chuckled.

Then she glanced down.

I followed her gaze—and gasped.

There was Ricky, hunched on the floor.

But he wasn't Ricky anymore.

He was a frog.

"Ribbit," he croaked. *"Ribbit. Ribbit."*

"You turned him into a *frog!*" Liv cried out in shock.

The old woman smiled. "I told you I know all sorts of tricks. Wasn't that a good one?"

She knelt down. She tickled the frog's head. "He's a cute frog, isn't he?"

We stood in shocked silence.

She narrowed her eyes at us. "Don't you think he's a cute frog?" she asked sharply.

I nodded. I didn't know what else to do.

"I knew you'd agree. He's a very cute frog." She tickled the frog's belly. "I hope he enjoyed being a boy for a few days."

"You mean—he was *never* a real boy?" I asked in disbelief.

"No. He was just a frog. A frog I turned into a boy for a little while."

The old lady gave the frog a final pat on the head. Then she straightened up and began pacing the room. "Now, let's see. Let's see."

She stopped pacing. She stared at us. Studied us. "Let's see . . . What shall I do with you two?"

I grabbed Liv's arm. I jumped up from the couch. "Let's *go!*"

We ran for the door.

We were halfway there when the old woman let out a soft giggle.

I turned to glance at her. She lifted her right hand high.

She drew three circles in the air and began to chant:

> *"Creature of prey.*
> *Creature of night.*
> *Watchful creature.*
> *Creature take flight!"*

"Hoooo!" The cry of an owl echoed through the room.

We heard the soft flutter of wings—and then we saw it.

The owl on top of the grandfather clock was alive! It shook out its wing feathers.

Then it took to the air.

It soared down at us.

Circled us.

It let out another sharp cry. Then it swooped toward my face with outstretched talons.

I threw my hands over my head. I tried to dodge it. But it kept coming at me. First from the left. Then from the right.

"Stop it! Stop it!" Liv cried out.

The owl dove for her. Grazed the top of her head.

It circled us, cutting off our escape. Forcing us back into the room.

"I see you've changed your minds." The old woman's lips parted into a satisfied smile. "You've decided to stay after all."

She raised her left hand—and the owl returned to its perch. Its wings fluttered one last time. Then the life flickered out of its eyes.

"Now . . . where was I?" The old woman rested her chin in the palm of her hand and gazed at us.

"Let us go!" I shouted.

"I'm sorry, but I can't do that," she replied.

"Why not?" Liv wailed. "We brought the bag back. What else do you want?"

"What else do I want?" the old woman asked. "Why, I want some new pets—of course. Now . . . what shall I turn you into?"

proached us slowly, swinging the trick-or-treat bag in her hand.

"Okay. Which one of you wants to go first?" she asked as she stepped up to us.

We didn't answer.

"Is somebody going to speak?" She shifted her gaze from Liv to me.

We remained silent.

"Fine. I'll choose." She lifted the bag—and started to lower it over my head.

"Better say good-bye to your friend now," she told me. "Because in a few seconds, you'll only be able to croak."

19

"Noooo!" I screamed.

I grabbed the old woman's shoulders. I tried to shove her away.

But she was too strong. She didn't lose her balance. Not even a tiny bit.

"Be still!" she commanded sternly.

And suddenly, I couldn't move! It was as if my arms were strapped to my sides. My legs rooted to the floor.

The old woman lowered the bag slowly over my head. And there was nothing I could do to stop her.

The fabric slid over my hair.

Over my forehead.

As she pushed the bag down, the old lady chanted a spell in a low voice.

My face grew warm. My skin began to tingle.

"Leave him alone!" Liv shouted. She kicked the woman hard in the shin.

"Owwww!" The old lady let out a startled cry and bent down to rub her leg.

The kick must have broken her concentration or something. Because suddenly I could move again. My hands shot up. I ripped the bag off my head.

"You can't escape me!" she snarled.

She started to straighten up—and I quickly slipped the bag over her head!

I yanked it down. Over her face. Over her chin. Down to her shoulders.

The old woman twisted inside the bag, struggling to break free.

"Hold her arms, Liv," I yelled as the old woman thrashed inside the bag. "Don't let her out!"

"You can't do this to me!" the woman shrieked.

She struggled harder.

She twisted her body fiercely, left and right. She squirmed and kicked.

She tried to grab for me, but Liv held her arms in place.

And then I lifted the bag from her head.

I let her out.

And, in what seemed like the blink of an eye, *two* identical old women stood before me.

20

"**O**h no!" Liv gasped. "There are two of them! How could you do this, Greg? How?"

"*He* didn't do anything." One of the old women leered. "*I* did it! Now there are two of us! Two of us—to get the two of you!"

The old women glared at us.

Their orange lips parted slowly.

"*Now!*" they both cried out—and lunged for us.

Liv and I bolted—but those old ladies were fast.

One chased Liv around the couch. The other reached out and grabbed for my arm. She caught my sleeve and tugged me toward her, hard.

"Give me that bag!" she screeched, groping for the trick-or-treat bag, which I held in my other hand.

"No!" I swung it behind my back, out of her reach.

The other woman caught Liv. She held her tightly. "*I* want that trick-or-treat bag!" she said. She glared at the woman who held me. "*You* wouldn't know what to do with it!" she screamed at her.

Then she shifted her gaze toward me. "Give it to me, boy," she said sweetly. "Give me the bag—and I'll let you go."

"Don't believe her!" Liv cried. "Don't give it to her! Don't let either of them have it!"

Would she really let us go? I wondered.

What should I do?

My head throbbed as the two women stared at me. Waiting. Waiting to see if I would give up the bag.

What should I do? What should I do? I asked myself.

Everyone's gaze remained on the bag.

What should I do? I asked myself again.

And, suddenly, I knew exactly what to do.

I held out the bag to the woman who held Liv.

"Are you *crazy?*" Liv screamed.

The old woman let Liv go and lunged for the bag.

"Noooo!" the woman who held me cried.

She pounced for the bag too—and let me go.

My plan worked! We were free!

I leaped back, out of reach of both women. They grabbed for me—but I wasn't there anymore. They crashed into each other and fell to the floor.

And I still held the trick-or-treat bag in my hand!

"Run!" I shouted to Liv.

We made it to the front door.

"Stop them!" I heard one of the women cry. "They're getting away with the bag!"

I tried to turn the doorknob.

It didn't move!

"Hurry!" Liv screamed. "They're coming!"

I tried to yank the door open.

It didn't budge.

"There must be another door!" Liv shouted. "We have to find it!"

We turned—and froze.

The two horrible old women stood before us, blocking our way.

Before I knew what was happening, one of them had reached out and snatched the bag from my grasp.

She turned to her twin. "Time for you to go!" she cackled.

She lifted the bag. She started to bring it down over the other old lady's head.

The other old lady grabbed my arm.

She shoved me in front of her.

And the bag came down—over *my* head!

21

"**W**hoops!" The old woman who held the bag giggled. She lifted it off my head.

I squeezed my eyes shut. I couldn't bear to look. "Am I okay?" I tried to ask Liv.

But all that came out was a long, loud *"Cluuuuck!"*

"Liv! What happened!" I tried to yell.

"Cluck! Cluck! Cluck!" came out of my mouth.

"Oh no! You turned him into a chicken!" Liv shrieked in horror.

My eyes popped open. I bent my head and stared at my body.

Feathers.

I was covered in reddish brown feathers.

"Cluck! Cluck! Cluuuuuck!" My beak quivered.

I glared up at the old woman who had done this to me. My head bobbed up and down as I pecked at her foot. I pecked hard!

"Turn me back!" I screamed at her.

But all that came out was, *"Cluck! Cluuuuck!"*

"What a nice chicken." She bent down and stroked my head. "I do love fresh eggs for breakfast!"

She ruffled my feathers—and Liv grabbed the bag from her!

She bolted across the room.

"Give that back to me!" the old woman shrieked.

"No! Give it to *me! Me!*" her twin yelled. "Give it to *me*—and I'll turn your friend back into a boy!"

"Don't make promises you can't keep. I'm the one with the magic, not you!" The old woman shoved her twin hard. "You have no magic. *I'm* the one with the power. *I'm* the one who knows the spells. I *made* you!"

I fluttered across the room to Liv. She scooped me up. She smoothed down my feathers and tucked me under her arm.

The old women were screaming at each other. One lunged for the other's throat. They wrestled each other to the floor.

"We're going to try to sneak out," Liv whispered to me. "I'm going to try to find another door."

She moved across the room slowly. Step by step. Trying not to attract any attention.

It wasn't hard. The old women didn't notice us. They were too busy tearing at each other's clothes. Pulling each other's hair.

Liv kept inching across the room. Slowly. Slowly.

I stared at the struggling old ladies.

One of the old women suddenly tore herself free and jumped up. "I'm going to finish you off," she panted, aiming a bony finger at her twin. She grabbed a pink crystal from a nearby table.

She held it in front of a candle's flame.

She stared into its warm, pink glow.

"Noooo!" the other woman shrieked. She leaped to her feet. Her eyes darted frantically around the room—searching, searching for something.

Then she found it—the book called *Magic*.

She picked it up and flipped madly through its pages.

At last she must have found the right page. She ran her finger down it, reading swiftly. Mumbling the words. Repeating them over and over. Memorizing them.

Liv took another step—and another. No one paid any attention to us.

The first old woman continued to stare deep into the crystal. She held it before the flame. She stared at it, in a trance. Then she began to chant:

"Glowing crystal, glowing bright,
Gathering strength in candlelight.
This old woman we will banish;
With your power, make her vanish—"

"Stop!" the other woman shrieked. She made a grab for the crystal.

Now they both held on to it tightly—and they both screamed out the last part of the chant:

"The one who holds the crystal near
Will make the other disappear!"

There was a moment of absolute silence. No one moved. No one breathed.

Even the clocks stopped ticking.

And then . . .

Both old ladies started to fade.

Liv froze in midstep.

We watched in amazement as their figures grew more and more transparent.

They faded and faded. In a few seconds we could see right through them.

And then they disappeared.

A loud *cluck* escaped from my throat—and my head started to hurt. It was stuck under Liv's armpit!

My head!

My real head!

The old ladies were gone—the spell was broken.

I was a kid again!

"Ow!" I cried. My voice was muffled against Liv's shirt. "Let go of me!"

Liv shrieked and threw her arms up. I stumbled free of her grasp.

"You're back!" Liv cheered. "Hooray!"

We charged for the front door and raced out of the house.

We ran all the way down Fear Street. Under the gnarled tree branches that blocked out the moonlight. Past the gloomy front yards. Past the crumbling houses.

We didn't stop running until we reached my house.

"I can't believe that happened," Liv panted. "I just can't believe it. I'm never going to Fear Street again. Never."

"*You* can't believe it!" I cried. "I turned into a chicken!"

For the first time all day, Liv laughed.

But her grin quickly faded when she saw what I held in my hand. Her green eyes flickered with fear.

"How did you get *that?*" She pointed at the trick-or-treat bag I held.

"I grabbed it off the floor when we ran out of the house. But don't worry about it," I told her.

"Don't worry about it!" Liv put her hands on her hips. "What do you mean, don't worry about it? You can't use it again! That bag is trouble! You have to get rid of it!"

"I know," I said. "That's why I took it. I'm going to bury it somewhere—a safe place where no one can find it."

"Promise?" Liv begged.

"I promise. I'm not going to use it. I've learned my lesson. It's much too dangerous. Really. I've learned my lesson. . . ."

22

Liv burst through our kitchen door. "Muffin is back!" she announced.

"Where?" My eyes darted around the kitchen, looking for him.

"Relax." Liv laughed. "He's in Mrs. O'Connor's front yard. I walked by him on my way over here. I guess he found his way home okay yesterday."

It was the next morning—the morning after our second visit to Fear Street. I guess I was still a little jumpy.

"Are you sure it was the real Muffin?" I asked, opening the cabinet under the sink.

"I'm sure." Liv took a seat at the table. "He wasn't

waddling, and he nearly bit my hand off when I tried to pet him."

Liv glanced at the table, where I had placed my sneakers. They were the sneakers I had worn to the garbage dump—and they were pretty filthy.

"Phew. You're not going to *wear* these, are you?" She held her nose. "They stink!"

"I know." I peered inside the cabinet. "I'm looking for something to use to clean them."

"I'm telling." I heard Raina's irritating voice from the doorway.

I pulled my head out of the cabinet. "You're telling *what?*"

"I'm telling Mom you put your sneakers on the table." She turned to Liv. "Mom says we're not supposed to put our shoes on the furniture."

"Hey, look who's here!" Liv glanced at the door. Princess sauntered in.

I watched Princess as she entered the kitchen.

Was she *our* Princess—or one of the copies?

I stretched out my hand to stroke her head.

"Don't touch her!" Raina screamed.

I jerked my hand back. "Why not?"

"Because she's *my* cat!" Raina scooped Princess up and left the room.

I let out a sigh.

Liv suddenly jumped up from her seat. She glanced nervously around the kitchen.

"What's wrong?" I asked.

"I just remembered. What happened to all the roaches?"

"They're gone. Mom called an exterminator to get rid of them," I explained. "But she's still pretty upset. I don't think her reading group is ever going to come back here."

"And what about the bag?" Liv continued to scan the room. "Did you hide the trick-or-treat bag?"

I nodded.

"Did you hide it where no one will find it?" she pressed.

"Uh-huh," I answered. "I buried it under some rocks in Shadyside Park." I paused. "But first—uh—first I used it one more time."

"What do you mean?" Liv's voice rose. "How could you! You promised!"

I didn't answer.

"What did you do with it?" She was shouting now.

"Calm down," I told her. "Come up to my room and I'll show you."

"I don't believe you," Liv mumbled, shaking her head, as we walked up the stairs. "After everything that happened—how could you use that bag!"

We walked down the hall to my bedroom. Liv squinted at me. "Why is the door closed?" she asked, twirling her braid around her fingers.

I didn't reply.

I just opened the door slowly.

Liv poked her head in the doorway—and shrieked!

23

"**H**i, Liv." One of the Gregs in my room waved to her. He sat on the floor, refolding my shirts.

When he was finished, another Greg organized them in my drawer by color.

A different Greg tucked the sheet under my mattress. Then he smoothed the blanket out on top—while another crawled under the bed with a feather duster.

My room was filled with Gregs. All together there were ten of me!

It was awesome to see!

"You made copies of yourself!" Liv stared at all the Gregs in disbelief. "What are they doing?"

"They're cleaning," I said. "They're like me—but not exactly. They're neat."

"We're finally going to beat Derek!" One of the Gregs cheered.

"Yes!" Another one pumped his fist in the air. "Ten Gregs and only one Derek!"

All the Gregs laughed.

"I've got to sit down." Liv walked over to my bed and plopped down. She looked sort of pale.

"This is the day, Liv!" I told her. "Today is my lucky day. Today is the day I win! There are ten of me—and only one of him! Derek will never beat that. Never!"

"From now on Greg will always be the winner!" another Greg declared.

"Oh, really?" Liv murmured. She was staring out my window. "Um—I wouldn't be so sure of that."

"Huh? What are you talking about?" I stepped up to the window.

I stared outside—and gasped.

There was Derek, marching up to my house.

In his hand he carried the magic trick-or-treat bag.

Next to him walked another Derek. And next to that Derek, another. And another. And another. . . .

I counted the Dereks—and screamed.

There were ten of me.

But there were *twenty* of him!

About R.L. Stine

R.L. Stine is the best-selling author in America. He has written more than one hundred scary books for young people, all of them bestsellers.

His series include *Fear Street, Ghosts of Fear Street* and the *Fear Street Sagas*.

Bob grew up in Columbus, Ohio. Today he lives in New York City with his wife, Jane, his teenage son, Matt, and his dog, Nadine.

R·L·STINE'S
GHOSTS of FEAR STREET ®

COLLECTOR'S EDITIONS

DO YOU DARE READ THEM ALL?

THE BEGINNING

The New Girl
The Surprise Party
The Overnight

NIGHTMARES

The Sleepwalker
The Secret Bedroom
Bad Dreams

SECRETS

The Confession
What Holly Heard
The Face

DANGEROUS GIRLS

The Rich Girl
The Dare
The Prom Queen

From Archway Paperbacks
Published by Pocket Books

1466-01